I0534207

Me, Myself and You

By Adrianna Cote

To my loving husband, an unexpected passenger that joined my journey. We met while we were both at a fork in the road and a new journey began, our journey. All my love.

Special Acknowledgements:
Chantal, Dianna, Dyane and Suzanne.
I have a novel that I am proud of and a dream come true.
Thank you for all you have done that brought me here.

Adrianna Cote

Table of Contents

Adrianna Cote

Chapter 1

Patricia placed the telephone receiver back in it's cradle. She placed her head in her hands and sighed. That was not a great call. She realized that maybe she needed to look at adding more personnel to the practice. Perhaps a security guard, they could dress in work attire to blend in.

Patricia practiced real estate law but took on the odd criminal case to keep her practice interesting. Her husband, James, had asked her over and over to give up practicing criminal law. He didn't like the risk she took dealing with people who quite possibly could harm another human being. Pat didn't care. She enjoyed the challenge of a tough case, and arguing to defend a client in open court was a rush. Pat just couldn't give it up.

They got into a very heated argument one night after one of Pat's client left her office yelling and screaming obscenities at Pat, threatening to kill her. James had to call in the police to have the client removed.

"What would you do if he made good on his threats?" James asked Pat.

Adrianna Cote

"James, please, he was upset that the court would not find in favour of him and is facing some serious jail time. Wouldn't you be upset too. It was all bark."

"I wish you would look at this from my perspective, you and Kate are all I have in this world, and if something happened to you, what would I do?" James asked.

"Baby, you watch too many movies, I am more likely to be hit by a car than to be harmed by a client," Pat returned, rolling her eyes.

James bowed his head in defeat, he knew he would never convince her to quit her criminal practice.

Pat feeling bad that he was so worried put her arms around James and pulled him close.

"Baby, you know I'll take you with me," Pat said nuzzling his nose.

James leaned in resting his forehead against hers, "Baby, you know I'll be by your side."

They embraced, feeling his arms around her filled her heart to the brim and she couldn't help but think how much she loved this man.

Pat cleared her thoughts and began thinking about the call she had just gotten. She pulled out the number of a company she had gotten from a client of hers. Pat knew that the client had needed these services at times and had asked him if he could provide a reliable contact for her. Pat had a feeling she might need it, but had put off making the call because she was worried she was overreacting.

Years ago, Pat had defended a criminal, named Henry. He had been charged with attempted murder and Pat was able to get the case dismissed on a technicality. A vital piece of evidence was unaccounted for 24 hours during the investigation. Meaning the chain of evidence was broken and anything could have happened to it during that time. Like planting false DNA, so, Pat could argue the evidence be dismissed from the prosecution's case. The prosecution did not have enough to convict Henry on what they had left and tried to broker a deal. Pat knew they had no case and refused to barter, causing the prosecution to ultimately abandon the charges and Henry was free to go live his life. Now there is a big difference between a case being dismissed and a person being innocent and Pat wondered if Henry was innocent. The reason Pat wondered was because Henry could be unstable at times and was difficult to deal with, but it wasn't Pat's place to decide if he was innocent or guilty. Nonetheless, Pat decided that once the matter was completed she would have nothing to do with Henry again.

So, when Henry showed up to her office requesting Pat defend his son, Kevin, who had been arrested and charged for drug and human trafficking. He was looking at many years behind bars. Pat had to stand by her decision and refuse the case. She told Henry that she was very busy and was not taking on any new clients at the time, which was not entirely false. Pat offered Henry the name of another lawyer but her refusal to take on Kevin's matter made Henry very upset. Henry stormed out of the office cursing and yelling out threats. He had slammed the door so hard that he had cracked the glass in the door. This reinforced Pat's decision to not continue a professional relationship with this man.

It had been a long time and Pat had actually forgotten about the whole incident with Henry, so when the lawyer Pat had recommended called her, she had to stop and recall who and why she had referred the matter. The lawyer, Dom, who had taken on the matter, had called Pat to let her know that the trial had not gone well. The Crown Attorney had won the case by a landslide, there was so much evidence against his client that Dom could barely keep his head above water while arguing the case. Ultimately Kevin was sentenced with two consecutive life sentences. Dom was calling Pat because he wanted to warn her about Henry's reaction to the sentence his son received.

Dom told Pat that Henry got very angry and started causing a scene in the courthouse. He blamed Dom for not doing a good job, and blamed Pat for not taking on the case. Henry believed that had Pat taken on the matter she would have gotten his son the same result that Pat had gotten Henry. Henry was escorted from the courthouse by two armed police officers, all the while, yelling out threats of serious harm to Dom and Pat. Dom told Pat that at the moment, Henry was in police custody for the threats and for disturbing the peace. Pat thanked Dom for the heads up and disconnected the call. She sat there for a moment unsure of what to do. Finally, her brain kicked into gear and she knew what her next step was.

Pat shuffled through some business cards she kept in a leather binder on her desk, flipping pages until she found the one she was looking for. It was for a security firm. She called and left a message with the firm that had been recommended by her client, but things weighed heavy on her. Pat had a very bad feeling about the whole situation and for some reason had a strong urge to write a letter to her daughter, Kate, just in case something did happen to her. Pat pulled out a pen and paper and began to write.

My dearest baby girl, Pat started to write and then paused. Pat wanted to write all that had happened and why she was writing the letter, she wanted to tell Kate how proud she was, how much joy she brought to Pat's life, how much she loved Kate. But Pat didn't want to upset Kate and she already knew how proud Pat was of her and how much she loved her because Pat told her that everyday. Pat tried to think about what things would look like for Kate if something did ever happen to her. Kate, being so much like her mother, loved deeply and lost deeply. So, Pat decided to write words that she hoped would bring Kate comfort in a time of need.

Once Pat finished her letter she placed it in a sealed white envelope and put it in her top drawer. Pat decided to try the security company again but just as she was about to pick up the phone a client walked around the corner towards her office carrying a large bouquet of flowers. Pat smiled knowing exactly who it was, and headed out to greet him.

Jordan, one of her favourite clients, poked his head out from behind the flower arrangement, smiling.

"Happy birthday Patty," Jordan said.

Jordan was the only one who called her Patty. Jordan was just a boy when he became a client of James'. Jordan was barely fourteen when his parents died in a tragic car accident, leaving Jordan the sole beneficiary of all their assets and acquisitions. Jordan learned very quickly that people were out to dethrone him from his position. James was Jordan's father's trusted attorney and Jordan turned to James to help him maintain his parent's legacy, and his birth right. James often turned to Pat for a second opinion on Jordan's matters. He wanted to be sure he was helping Jordan because it made him angry to think of people out there taking advantage of this vulnerable young man.

Pat's relationship with Jordan quickly went from professional to Pat treating and feeling like Jordan was more a son to her than client. Jordan returned Pat's fondness and would rely on both James and Pat more and more, often not being business related.

"Thank you, Jordan, they are beautiful," Pat said happily.

Pat's day being so hectic, and with the added stress of Henry's outburst, she had forgotten it was her birthday. They began to talk about current events, both at a loss for words when it came to the presidential candidates vying for election. They laughed at the absurdity should the one candidate win the election.

"I absolutely believe we should build a wall," Jordan said laughing, "not to keep us in but to keep him out."

They began to talk about their plans for the evening. Pat has been trying to get Jordan to come to the house for dinner for many years, but he, much like her daughter, was a "home body", never venturing out much. Pat finally managed to convince Jordan to join their family for Christmas dinner, but a snow storm blew in and the roads were closed, so he never came.

"Jordan, please join us for dinner tonight. It's going to be very simple. We are going to get takeout from my favourite Japanese restaurant and have a quiet celebration at the house. I would really love it if you could finally meet Kate," Pat asked, trying again.

"I'm not sure Pat," Jordan replied showing his discomfort by shifting his weight, "I do have plans with Todd tonight."

Pat chuckled, "A boys' night? You can do that anytime. I only turn 49 once," she paused and added, "bring him, I would love for Kate to be around people her own age rather then keeping her nose glued to a book. Pllleeeaaassseee," she begged.

Jordan stood quiet for a moment. He looked deep in thought but after a few minutes he looked at Pat and smiled, nodding in agreement. Pat clapped her hands with joy and then gave Jordan a hug. She couldn't be happier. Pat wanted Jordan and Kate to meet. She just loved them both so much it felt wrong that Kate and Jordan didn't know each other.

They confirmed the time and were just about to say their goodbyes when they heard James from the other room, yelling. It was unlike James to be yelling and Pat couldn't make out his words. As soon as she heard the loud bang resonate through the office, she knew what James had yelled, "gun."

Pat froze at the sound of the bang, unsure if James had been hit. She didn't know if she should run to James or run for the phone to call the police. Either way it didn't matter she could not seem to convince her feet to move.

Within seconds, the gunman rounded the corner, pointing the barrel of the gun directly at Jordan. Pat's instinct kicked in causing her to push Jordan out of the way to shield him from the gunman. Just as she did she felt the bullet tear through her abdomen, she felt the pain before she even heard the shot. Pat fell to the floor but scrambled to shield Jordan from harm.

Pat looked up at the gunman, she recognized him right away. It was Henry. Apparently, he had come to make good on his threats. Henry pointed the barrel of the gun at Jordan. Pat knew he would pull the trigger.

Pat put up her hand, "No," she said to Henry in a very shaky voice.

The gunman turned his attention and the gun back to her and as a small smile spread across his face he pulled the trigger again. The bullet hit not very far from the first one. Pat began feeling very weak but she didn't feel very much pain. She couldn't decide if that was a good thing or a bad thing. She closed her eyes for a moment trying to find strength. She slowly opened her eyes and as she did she could hear sirens in the distance. The gunman began retreating slowly but before long he was tearing out of the office to avoid arrest.

"Oh, my goodness! Patty!" Jordan called out grabbing Pat and pulling her into his arms. She felt very weak and could hardly move but she had to know what happened to James.

Pat knew that the sirens meant that James hit the alarm. Maybe he was ok.

"James?" Pat whispered, pointing for Jordan to go check.

Jordan nodded, placing her gently back on the floor he ran to the other office and back in what felt like a blink of an eye. Which could have been minutes with how weak and tired she felt. It was a struggle to keep her eyes open.

Pat could tell from the look on Jordan's face that James had been shot by the gunman and had been killed. Pat let out a sob, but the only sound that escaped was a gurgle. She fought to gain control and enough strength to get through the next few minutes, she had a feeling she would be with James soon.

"Jordan," Pat said choking on her words, "there's an envelope in my desk, top drawer. Please see that Kate gets it."

Pat could feel a warm liquid starting to seep out of her mouth and she had a feeling it was red. She closed her eyes feeling so very tired, but was shaken by Jordan causing her to open her eyes.

"No Patty, you hang on, you're going to be okay, you have to be okay," Jordan cried.

"Maybe, but just in case. You have to give her the letter. Kate has no one, Jordan. I need you to be there for her, just as we have been there for you," she finished.

"You're going to be okay, you're going to be okay," Jordan repeated over and over again, rocking Pat in his arms.

Pat placed her hand on Jordan's cheek, causing him to stop, "Promise me Jordan," she pleaded. She needed to know Kate was going to be taken care of.

Jordan nodded.

"You're such a good boy. Sorry you're a man, but you will always be that little boy to me. James and I loved you, you are..." Pat's words trailed off.

Pat felt very tired, and could not keep Jordan in focus no matter how hard she tried. She wanted to hold on. She wanted to fight to be with Kate and Jordan, but she wanted to be with James and James was dead. She could feel James' presence. James, she thought, that's where she belonged, at his side, in his arms.

Pat knew Jordan would take care of Kate. She knew she could go and be with James. "You know, I'll take you with me," Pat said her voice strong and clear, although she could not be sure if she said the words out loud.

"You know, I'll be by your side," Pat heard in return.

Pat never dreamed that James would be by her side in this moment, but she was thankful he was.

Pat lost all focus of the outside world, she could hear James calling for her, his voice was sweet music and she had to follow it. She closed her eyes and gave into the music knowing very well that she would never open her eyes again.

Chapter 2

Lying there staring up at the ceiling, Kate's eyes were burning from crying all night and lack of sleep. She couldn't bring herself to crawl out of bed this morning. Her chest felt like a cinder block was dropped on it, her breath short and rapid. The pain at times was unbearable. Kate curled up into the fetal position trying to relieve some of the pain without any luck. She broke out again into hysterical cries.

"Why? Why me? Why Now? I need you here!" she yelled to the empty room. Kate cried until she had no tears left, her emotions turned numb, which suited her fine. It was the only way she was going to get through this day. She finally pulled herself off the bed and began to get ready to say good bye.

It wasn't long before she heard a knock on the front door. Kate dreaded opening it because it brought her that much closer to the hardest thing she has ever had to do in her life. The knock came again. Kate slowly went to the door and opened it. There stood Charlie and his wife. Charlie was her parent's attorney. They looked at Kate with such pity. Kate hated that look.

"How are you dear?" asked Charlie's wife.

Seriously? Kate thought, how am I? Is this woman daft?

"Goodness, Martha, what a silly thing to ask," Charlie spat at his wife.

Martha, looked at Kate with an apologetic glance, making Kate feel bad for her. Martha was only trying to be nice.

"It's fine Charlie, thank you for your concern Martha," Kate said.

"Well, shall we go?" asked Charlie.

What's the rush? Kate thought to herself. It's not like they're going anywhere. This made her tears begin to fall again. All Kate could do was shake her head yes.

They all got into Charlie's car and pulled out of the driveway. The trip there was quiet. Charlie had the radio playing very softly and no one spoke a word. Kate didn't know how long it took them to get to the cemetery, her concept of time was completely out of wack.

There were a few people already at the grave site and everyone rushed to give their condolences to Kate. Kate was feeling very overwhelmed so she pulled herself away from the other mourners and took her seat. The funeral was a blur. Kate didn't care what anyone had to say about her parents. All that mattered was what she had to say to her parents and Kate would never get that chance.

Kate sat there looking at the two caskets side by side each with a large flower arrangement on the top. It was surreal to think her parents were in them and that they were about to bury them under, what, 6 feet of dirt? That realization caused her tears to flow once more.

Once the ceremony was over everyone wanted to help Kate and offered to stay with her. She thanked them and asked them to go on to the luncheon. She needed some time alone. Kate said she would find her way over in a little bit but Kate knew there was no way she was going to sit in a hall with a bunch of people eating and talking about how her parents use to be.

Once alone Kate stepped back and let the workers do their job. She watched as they lowered one coffin into the ground, her father, and they buried him with soil then they placed her mother's coffin on top of her fathers and finished filling the hole. They laid out fresh sod, moved all the flowers to the headstone and left. Kate walked over to her parent's headstone and knelt onto the ground.

The sun was hot on the back of her neck. She kneeled on the freshly laid sod for a long time, her head bowed and tears streaming down her face. She could not seem to get herself to stand. She just wanted to curl up on the ground right here and never get up.

Kate lifted her head and looked at the grey marble stone, the words blurring from her tears but she knew what it said,

Adrianna Cote

Here Lies:
Patricia Black
Born March 6, 1969
Died March 6, 2014
"Baby, you know I'll take you with me"
And
James Black
Born July 29, 1965
Died March 6, 2014
"Baby, you know I'll be by your side"

Kate could hear them saying those words to each other and her heart broke again, and so began another sobbing fit.

Her parents never said the traditional "I love you". Kate asked her mom one time why they would say such a morbid thing. Her mom's reply was your dad knows I love him in this life, but I want him to know that I will love him in the next. So instead of reminding him how much I love him now, I remind him of how I will love him if I leave this world without him. Kate's mom paused and sighed sadly and said your dad's response tells me how he won't be able to live without me.

Kate sobbed again, "Why, why now? You're supposed to grow old together, see me marry, or not marry," she said angrily at the headstone. Defeated she continued, "How do I move on from here? Who do I have if I don't have you?" Kate meant that literally, her parents were only children, as were their parents who also passed away before their time.

"Who do I have?" Kate said again.

"Miss. Black?" Someone spoke her name. Kate did not recognize the voice so she turned her face up to the sun. It was a man, his body shaded the sun so it didn't hurt her eyes. She recognized him from the bail hearing of the appalling man who put her parents in the ground, but her head was in a fog and Kate could not recall his name for the life of her. She knew the man was the client in her parent's office when they died but nothing more. Why was he here? She wanted to be alone.

"Go away," Kate instructed, turning back to the headstone.

"I do apologize for the intrusion," his voice strong and gruff, "I am very sorry for what you are going through, I knew your parents well and they were good people."

Kate looked back to the man and noticed he held an envelope in his hand, just as she did he held it out to her. "Your mother asked that I give this to you."

Hesitating to reach for the envelope, Kate looked this man over once more. He was average height for a man, with broad shoulders. His baldhead gleamed in the sun. He was not old, late twenties, maybe, the lack of hair suited him, like it did her father. This reminder of her father made her heart skip a beat. The man's stance was strong and confident. But his eyes, they were blue with a hint of sliver, and they were mesmerizing and warm.

Kate took the white envelope and held it in her hands. Did she want to know what it said? Yes, and no. If she didn't read it, it would haunt her for the rest of her life. If kept sealed, it would leave Kate with the notion that her mom still had one more thing to say to her, making Kate feel like her mom wasn't quite gone. These were her mother's words. She knew she had to know what it said, so she opened it.

The man took a few steps back but did not leave. Seriously! Why was he still here? Kate thought.

She ignored him and began to read:

My dearest baby girl,

You will find a way to move on, I know you will…. One foot in front of the other.

You know I'll take you with me.

Love mom

An answer to the question Kate just asked the headstone. Kate was shocked, even in death her mom knew her too well. But a note? It was like her mom knew that she was going to die. Her sobbing began again. The stranger just stood there waiting. Kate's sobbing subsided and she looked at the note one more time before she folded it and put it back in the envelope. She steadied herself to stand and as she did the man held out his hand to help her to her feet.

His hand was warm, strong and gave Kate comfort, which was weird given she did not know this man at all.

She looked at him quizzically, "Why are you still here?" she asked.

"Your mom asked me to help you, and be there for you until you were on your feet," he replied.

This struck her as odd.

He saw the confusion on her face and offered an explanation. "I was there that tragic day when your parents were killed and she asked me in her final moments."

Yes, Kate knew that, but that didn't answer the question of why he was still here. She looked at him and tried a different question, "Can you tell me what happened?" She asked.

He looked at her for a beat, then replied, "You know what happened. Your parents were shot by one of your mother's criminal client's."

"Yes, I know, but I want to know the details, no, I need to know the details," she demanded.

He shifted his weight and pulled at the collar of his shirt showing his discomfort. "I don't want to cause you further pain," he whispered.

"Further pain?" she said laughing angrily. "My parents are dead and I have no one else in this world to turn to. How much worse can it get?" Without waiting for a response, she continued, "You were there, you saw it all, tell me!" she demanded again.

He shifted his weight again and put his hands in his pocket and Kate could tell he was defeated.

"Alright, I do understand, I felt the same way once, but the truth still hurts, and in the end, they're still gone. Are you sure you want to know?" he asked.

Kate just gave him a nod.

"Perhaps we should sit," he suggested, pointing to a wooden bench not far from where they stood.

They walked over to a bench that looked over a hillside of the graveyard. This was a beautiful spot and it brought some comfort to Kate to know her parents had that view even if they'd never see it. Once seated, the man who last saw her parents alive, began to speak words she wished she'd never have to hear. Kate's heart ached and throbbed, knowing this was going to be bad, but she had to know her parent's final moments, even if it would scar her for the rest of her life.

Chapter 3

The man sat with his hands clasped, rolling his thumbs one over the other. Kate sat patiently and waited for him to begin. He cleared his throat and looked out into the distance.

"It was your mother's birthday," he began, "and like I always do, I brought her an arrangement of flowers. Your father has been my attorney for fourteen years, ever since my own parents left me orphaned. I struggled to keep my inheritance after my parent's death, and your parents saw to it that I kept what my parents had left me. We worked diligently together for days and weeks to maintain my inheritance. Before long your parents became surrogate parents to me. I started going to them for advice on everything. They were so patient and kind and always there to help me, and a lot of times not billing in the process. Your mother would handle my real estate and," he paused, "love life," he muttered. "Your dad dealt with all my business and acquisitions."

Adrianna Cote

Kate knew her parents both practiced different types of law. Her dad was a black and white person so it made sense that he liked business law, with all the contracts and proposals. Her mom was a bit more free-spirited but was convinced to perform in an area of law that would be profitable. So, her mom handled real estate deals but she needed to keep herself challenged, so she would take on a criminal case every once in a while. It didn't matter that her parents practiced different types of law. They enjoyed working together so they purchased a building downtown, renovated it and created Black Legal.

"Your mom and I were talking about her plans for the evening when we heard your dad yell out. I didn't hear the words clearly but soon knew what he had said. Once I heard the shot I knew your dad had been trying to warn us about the gunman. But I realized too late, the gunman was already running towards us."

He paused, and looked over at Kate and then back down at his hands.

"Your mom pushed me to the ground at the same time I heard the second shot. I had banged my head off the chair on my way down and then your mom landed on the ground beside me. My head was so fuzzy from the chair that it took me too long to realize what was happening. I didn't know your mom had been shot. The gunman came over to us and pointed the barrel of the gun at me and your mom put up her hand and told him "no". At that moment, he lost interest in me and turned the gun back to your mom," again the man paused. "He shot her again," the man whispered.

Kate could hear the anguish in his words. She knew her mom was shot twice but it still hurt her to hear.

"I thought he would turn back to me but just as the third shot came, we heard the sirens start. I guess your dad had hit the alarm button under his desk before he was shot." The man paused for a minute and looked down. She could see the grief on his face. "Then the gunman turned and fled leaving me alive," the last part he said in a hushed voice.

"Once the gunman was gone, I frantically checked your mom, she looked at me, she was stronger and calmer then I was and she asked me to go check on your dad. I did and found him in his office but he was already gone. Please don't ask me how I know. I went back to your mom but I didn't have to say a word, she could tell from the look on my face that your dad was gone. Your mom told me about an envelope in the top drawer of her desk and asked me to get it and give it to you. Then she asked me to stay with you until you were on your feet," he said and ran his hand over his cheek and gazed off into the distance like he was remembering something.

Then he turned and looked at her and said. "I will do as she wished whether it be literally," he said nodding towards where he had just helped Kate get on her feet just minutes before, "or figuratively".

"Did you know the gunman? Had you seen him around my parent's office before?" Kate asked.

"No, I had never seen him and only learned his name after," he replied.

She knew the name of the gunman. Henry was one of mom's criminal clients who was mentally ill, and snapped after his own son was sent to prison. He believed that had her mom taken his son on as a client then he wouldn't be in jail. Henry had no remorse. An eye for an eye was his defence in court.

It shook her to the core hearing this deranged man blaming her mom for something that was beyond her mom's control. Kate's life was changed forever because of this man, and she wanted him to pay for what he did. Just after the bail hearing Kate found out that Henry might go free.

The Prosecutor told Kate that Henry's lawyer was trying to say he was mentally incapacitated and should be given treatment not jail time. Just remembering this conversation angered her. She could feel the heat rising-up her neck and into her face.

Out of the corner of her eye she could see the man shifting on the bench and began to shake his leg anxiously. Kate realized her anger must be apparent and that he must think she is angry with him. She buried that thought deep in her mind, that would be dealt with when the time came. Kate got her anger under control.

"Thank you for telling me. You're right, they are still gone but at least my imagination can cease to run away with other terrifying ideas of my parent's last moments," she said.

He nodded, and she saw his body relax.

"Can I take you somewhere? I mean, can I give you a lift home? Unless you drove yourself here today?" he stammered.

No, she hadn't drove herself here today. Charlie, had driven her. He said it was part of his duty to her parents, but everyone looked at Kate with such pity, including Charlie and his wife, and she just needed everyone to go away. Kate had figured she would just walk home, or grab a bus, now realizing how bad that plan was.

The day's events had left her feeling very weak and suddenly she felt very tired. It was Sunday and busses didn't run on Sunday's. She could call a cab, with the cell phone she left at the bottom of the lake. It found its way there after about the fifth condolence call. So, her option was a very difficult trek home or accept this man's offer of a ride.

Kate nodded, "Thank you, that would be great."

They stood from the bench and she followed his lead. They headed towards the road where his car was parked. Once they got to his car it occurred to her that she still had not gotten this man's name and she was about to get into his car.

"Um, I should probably get your name before I get into a car with you," Kate said and offered him a slight smile.

"Jordan Best," he replied returning her smile.

They looked at each other for a moment, holding the stare a bit longer then you normally would. Kate began to feel strange so she broke the trance by turning and climbing into his car. He did as well. He fumbled around in his pockets looking for his keys, finally managing to pull them out, he put them in the ignition and turned. The car came to life, Jordan, put the car into gear and headed to the mouth of the cemetery. Kate looked back one more time at her parent's final resting place. Tears began to fall silently down her face. He reached over her and opened the glove box and produced a package of Kleenex. She nodded with a laugh, "You came prepared."

She accepted the tissues dabbing at her face.

Jordan pulled the car out onto the street and steered them in the direction of her house. The ride was quiet. All she heard was the sound of the tires on the road and the odd car horn. Even though she sat the entire ride staring out the window, she didn't recall the way they took to get home and was surprised to already be pulling into her drive. Shouldn't things take longer now? Kate thought to herself. Everything else seemed to move at a snail's pace.

Kate looked to the front door of the house. The front door to the house that she had spent the last twenty-four years living in with her parents. Kate found herself for the third time today unable to move. How could she walk through that door knowing her parents were not on the other side to greet her?

Kate looked over at Jordan who was also staring at the front door, he noticed she was looking at him and turned to her.

"I will sit here for as long as you need," was all he said.

He turned back to the steering wheel, and sat back in his seat to relax. Jordan did in fact look prepared to wait. Then she remembered him saying he was orphaned, so he gets it she thought to herself. Kate was relieved to have someone who understood how she felt.

They sat in silence as time ticked on. Cars passed, children rode by on their bikes, the neighbour was out walking his dog. She saw him pause on the sidewalk looking into the car watching. He was probably waiting for her to get out so he could tell her how sorry he was for her loss. Kate did not want to speak to anyone else today so she ignored him. After a few minutes, he continued his walk.

Finally, after what felt like hours she found the strength to move forward and she removed her seatbelt. It was the first step for Kate to walk through the front door to the awaiting silence that was to be her life. Kate saw Jordan become alert to her movements and he looked to her, his eyes asking if she was ready. She nodded and they both got out of the car. Jordan walked Kate to the front door and he waited as she unlocked the door, but she couldn't turn the knob.

Kate turned and put her back against the door, feeling the cool metal through her clothing. She closed her eyes and took a deep breath. She opened her eyes and saw him looking at her, this handsome kind man, who had gone out of his way to help her on one of the worst days of her life, and why? Because her mom had asked him to. Not just any person would follow through on that. She's not sure she would be able to if asked. She probably would have booked it the minute the ceremony was over to avoid the awkwardness of a grieving person.

But here he stood unmoving, waiting patiently. Kate wasn't sure why but she held out her hand for his, and he took hers without hesitation.

"You've been very kind, thank you. For a moment, I did not feel alone. I know I should thank you and let you be on your way but I'm not that gracious. I'm actually quite selfish, and so being true to form, could I ask one more thing of you?" Kate asked.

"Anything," Jordan replied.

"Would you please come inside with me and sit with me until I....," Kate trailed off, "well I don't know how long," she finished.

Jordan's response was not in words. He just stepped up onto the stoop of her house and took the lead by opening the

Adrianna Cote

front door with a gentle push. Jordan gave her a comforting smile and motioned for her to go in first. Kate took a deep breath and stepped over the threshold and into the darkness of her new life, neither of them realizing that from this day on they would always be together.

Chapter 4

$\mathcal{K}$ate and Jordan became very good friends, they found they had a lot in common and it all began with their love for her parents. True to his word Jordan would check in with Kate every day, whether it was a visit to the house or a telephone call that lasted for hours. Everyday Kate hoped Jordan would come to the house and would be disappointed if he only called her. Kate knew she felt something special with Jordan but she didn't realize that she was falling in love with him.

Kate struggled with living in her house. The memory of her parents everywhere. Eventually, Kate decided that maybe it was time for her to get her own apartment and start fresh. She tried discussing it with Jordan but he thought everything was moving too fast, and for her to make that kind of decision right now would be a bad idea. He insisted she wait a little while longer, but the longer she was in the house the harder it became to function. Kate found herself staying in her room for as long as she could so she wouldn't have to walk by her parent's room to go downstairs. She hated going out to the back yard because she could see them sitting on the outside couch, her mom's legs draped over her dad's, both reading some law article. She hadn't eaten at the kitchen table since before her parents died. Kate tried to get out of the house, to get away from the memory of them, but she could only get as far as the sidewalk before she realized she had nowhere to go.

It was late Monday night and Kate was feeling low. Jordan hadn't stopped by and he hadn't called her either. She wondered if he was getting bored with her, that he had fulfilled his duty to her mother. Kate wasn't much of a drinker but every once in a while, she liked to have a glass of wine with her mom. Her mom and dad rarely drank, so it wasn't something they had much of in the house.

Kate went on the hunt to find some wine. Her mom must have some tucked away somewhere. Kate found nothing. The only thing she found was a bottle of tequila in the bottom drawer of her dad's desk. It must have been a gift from someone because it still had a ribbon on it. There was a worm floating around the bottom of the bottle. Kate chuckled she could not see her dad drinking that, hence why it was in the bottom of his desk. It would have to do.

Kate never had tequila before and had to do a web search on how to drink it. She decided to try it straight up. After two shots, the burn of the alcohol felt good. After her third shot she found some courage and she called Jordan.

"Hello?" answered Jordan.

"Hey, it's Kate, you didn't call me," Kate replied.

"Kate, hey. Yeah, sorry, work was crazy. I was just walking in the door. I figured it was too late to call now," Jordan responded.

"Oh, I thought you were done with me," Kate said surprised at her straightforwardness.

"Why would you think that?" Jordan asked.

"I don't know, I'm really needy, and I really can't be here anymore," Kate replied again, clearly not filtering her thoughts.

"Um, are you ok?" Jordan asked.

"Sure, no worse than I was five minutes ago, you're right it's late. I'll talk to you later," Kate said and hung up without waiting for a response.

Kate placed the phone down and realized her heart was racing. She headed to the bottle and took one more shot of tequila. Kate realized that the fourth shot was not a great idea and went from feeling floaty to feeling like she was under a heavy see-through blanket. It was hard to walk and she couldn't keep her mind focused on anything. Kate thought maybe she should go lay down, but just as she was about to, there was a knock at the door. Who could be here at this hour? She wondered.

Kate stumbled to the door and opened it. There stood Jordan on the stoop.

"What are you doing here?" Kate asked, her speech slurring as she spoke.

"I was worried about you. You didn't seem yourself on the phone." Jordan told her and stared at Kate with a lifted eyebrow, "Are you drunk?" he asked.

"Drunk," Kate repeated laughing and then paused, oh man she thought, I am drunk. Kate had never had more than one drink before, so she had no idea that this is what was happening. "I think I might be," she whispered to Jordan.

"I see," Jordan said, "May I come in?"

"Sure," Kate said swinging the door wide open and stumbled back into the kitchen. She threw herself on a stool, struggling to keep her balance. "Okay, so I have never been drunk before and I wasn't really trying to get drunk. I just wanted to take the edge off. How does one get undrunk?" Kate asked Jordan.

Jordan laughed, "Time, and pizza," he told her. "I have not eaten and am starving and you look like you could use something greasy."

Kate thought about it and realized that sounded amazing. "Huh," Kate said, "How did you know that?"

"Well, I have had a few similar nights," he replied laughing.

Kate like how he laughed and she wanted to touch his lips. She thought, why do I want to touch his lips? She watched Jordan call for a pizza and he handed her a glass of water.

Jordan lifted the bottle of tequila, "So how many of these have you had?" he asked.

Kate pointed to the glass on the counter, "Four of those," she replied.

Jordan raised an eyebrow at her, "Really? Full or half the glass?"

"Full, why?" Kate asked.

"Well, because that glass is a double, so you would have had eight shots of tequila," Jordan responded.

Eight shots of tequila sure did seem like a lot more than four. No wonder she was so off, but she was getting used to the feeling and was starting to like it. She felt strong and brave, like she could do anything, touching Jordan's lips for example. Again, why was she thinking about his lips?

It wasn't long before the pizza got there. She ate three slices, it tasted better than any pizza she had ever had. She and Jordan talked about random things but eventually it came around to how she was doing.

The alcohol was wearing off and she was beginning to feel more like herself. Her thoughts were clearer too.

"I know you think that I should wait but I really have to get out of here. I am not going to sell but I need a fresh start, these walls are caving in on me," Kate told Jordan.

"It's up to you and I can understand why you would want to but I think you will regret doing it so soon," Jordan paused, "I have an idea. I must go out of town for a few weeks on business so my place will be empty. Why don't you take over the spare room while I am gone? Get some space and then at the end make a decision about what you want to do," he offered.

That did sound good Kate thought. Then she could take some time to look for a place and still get out of here.

"Are you sure?" Kate asked.

"Absolutely," Jordan said.

"That would be great," Kate agreed.

Kate had packed her bags and was at Jordan's place the very next day. Jordan showed her around and let her get settled. He left that evening for his trip. Kate felt good being out of the house but she was disappointed that she would not see Jordan for two weeks. He had some wine in a little cellar in his kitchen and Kate decided that she would have a glass. Just as she polished off the glass Jordan came walking into the house.

"Did you forget something?" she asked.

"No, my trip has been postponed," he responded eyeing the empty glass in Kate's hand.

Kate laughed, "I have only had one," she told him.

He smiled. "Well then I think I may have one as well, nothing like being stuck in an airport for three hours and not getting on a plane to put you in the mood for a drink," he said.

Jordan poured Kate another glass and himself one. They sat at the kitchen counter and talked while Kate kept thinking about how badly she wanted to touch his lips, and this time she couldn't blame the alcohol because she had barely even touched her second glass.

"Is everything okay, you seem like your miles away," Jordan asked.

"No, I am right here. I just keep thinking of something I want to do, that's all," Kate replied.

"Oh, we have that in common, I keep thinking about something I would like to do too," Jordan confided.

Kate laughed, "I really don't think we are thinking about the same thing," she said.

"Maybe not, but I think I may do what I want anyway," Jordan replied.

"Sure, knock yourself out," Kate said with a wave of her hand.

Jordan grinned ear to ear and then grabbed Kate's stool and pulled her right between his legs and planted his lips on hers before she even realized what was happening. Once Kate's brain caught up she was elated. He did want to do the same thing she did. Kate returned Jordan's kiss. That kiss led to many more over the next few days, weeks and months. Kate no longer a guest sleeping in the guest room, called Jordan's place home.

Two years later Kate still could not believe one of the worst days of her life gave her one of the best things to ever happen to her. It was her parent's death that brought Jordan into her life and as much as she missed her parents she was so thankful to have him.

Jordan's arm felt warm and safe wrapped around Kate's body. His face was turned in and nestled against her neck. She could feel the heat of his breath and the bristle of his five o'clock shadow scratching her skin. It sent shivers through her body. They swayed back and forth just being in each other's arms, the music playing softly in the background.

Jordan trailed kisses from the base of her neck softly and slowly until he reached the back of her ear causing Kate to groan softly with pleasure. His grip tightened on her body, she felt like she could hardly breathe.

"I don't think we are dancing to the beat of the song my love," Kate whispered not wanting to break the spell.

"Hmm, is there music?" Jordan responded as he gently rubbed his stubble cheek against her neck, sending shivers through her body again. Then he started to hum along to the radio, once the chorus hit he sang "Every little thing she does is magic," Jordan laughed quietly into her neck.

"You're funny," chuckled Kate, then chanted, "I put a spell on you."

Jordan leaned back and looked into her eyes, "You do bewitch me Ms. Black," he said wriggling his eyebrows. "When you're in my arms I'm spellbound. There is no one else but you."

Kate saw in his eyes, the love he had for her. It was all consuming. It made her heart ache just a little and she hoped that her love for him mirrored in her eyes. This man deserved all the love she had.

Jordan must have seen the worry on her face.

"What is it?" he asked.

Kate smiled. "I just don't ever want to lose this," she said.

Jordan smiled in return, nuzzling his nose against hers, "Where am I going?" he asked rhetorically. "So how was your day?" he asked, changing the subject.

"Was there a time before I was in your arms? I cannot recall," Kate replied, with a look of pure innocence on her face.

Jordan dipped her and kissed her chest just above her heart, then he looked into Kate's eyes.

"Good answer," he replied.

Then his smile shifted to a sly smile and he let her go.

Kate's breath caught in her chest, she prepared for the floor to meet her from behind but just as soon as Jordan let her go she hit something soft. Kate looked to the side and saw she had landed on the couch. Kate didn't even notice that Jordan danced them from across the room to this spot.

Jordan leaned over Kate, seeing the look of surprise on her face and chuckled.

"Baby, do you think I would ever do anything to hurt you?"

No, Kate knew he wouldn't. She smiled at him and grabbed the collar of his shirt and yanked Jordan towards her. He lost his balance and fell on top of her.

"Well, that same can't be said about me," she smiled coyly at him.

Adrianna Cote

Kate saw the blacks of Jordan's pupils dilate and retract with recognition, then his breath became staggered, his body tensed. His hand moved to cradle her head and shifted to lift the weight of his body from hers. Kate closed her eyes and groaned missing the lack of his weight against her, but her groan was muffled by Jordan's mouth covering hers.

Jordan kissed her gently, then more passionately. Before long his lips were greedy with want. He let his weight go and Kate felt the weight of him once more. She felt Jordan's body change and grow between her legs. Jordan pushed his groin into hers making her feel the bulk of him.

Kate moaned, wanting to rip those darn pants off him. Her hands gripping the back of his shirt pulling him hard against her, Kate released his shirt to find the button on his jeans. Just as she was about to free him, Jordan grabbed her wrists and brought them above her head. Holding her there as his other hand slowly moved down to find the bottom of her shirt.

Jordan's hand was hot on her skin and moved up her torso until he found the front closure of her bra. He unclipped it with ease and began gently cupping her breast running a finger over her nipple as he did. Kate moaned again and thrust her pelvis into his.

Jordan's desire grew, as did Kate's. He released her arms and they began hungrily removing each other's clothes until they were skin to skin. Jordan kissed Kate on the lips, then he trailed kisses down her face and neck, continuing to her breasts one side then the other pulling her nipples into his mouth. Kate's desire becoming overwhelming.

She had pins and needles on her tongue, she wanted him so badly. Jordan returned to her lips. They were both breathing heavy. Kate spread her legs, pulling her knees up and wrapping her legs around the back of his. Her fingers digging into the soft tissue of his very firm butt. Jordan adjusted himself until he met her opening and then he thrust in, moaning with pleasure as he did.

Everything became incoherent and all that mattered in that moment was him and the carnal pleasure that come from their two bodies colliding with one another. How Kate loved to hear him moan, the heat of his breath on her face and neck. She returned Jordan's thrusts with ones of her own, the pleasure built and built until she was crying out with every thrust.

Jordan's thrust came quicker until Kate became undone and cried out one last time, this time calling out his name. She could feel her body clenching around his manhood and this sent Jordan into overdrive. His thrusts hard and fast until she felt him exploding inside her, his body tensing, one final thrust and Jordan collapsed on top of her.

"Okay, that never gets old," Jordan said between heavy breaths.

Kate laughed and wrapped her arms around him and she thrust her pelvis into his again. Jordan's body spasmed and his breath caught. He pushed her pelvis away laughing too.

"Stop it, that tickles!" he commanded.

So, for good measure Kate did it one more time. Jordan groaned and flipped her so Kate was sitting on top of him, his hands on either side of her hips. He held her tight.

"Now you can't do that again," Jordan said smiling.

"Is that a challenge?" Kate asked raising one eyebrow at him.

Without waiting for a response, she began to rock her hips just a little because his grip was very tight. Jordan grunted a few times, his grip tightened and his body tensing with every rock of her hips.

"Stop, stop!" he cried out.

Kate didn't listen she continued to rock until she felt him grow hard inside her and Kate moaned. Jordan's grip lessened and his body relaxed.

"Ok, so don't stop," he groaned.

They both laughed and they made love again, falling asleep after, spent. Kate lying on his chest and his body still inside hers.

Chapter 5

The sun was shining into Kate's room, the brightness on her face woke her. She opened her eyes and sat up, the blanket clinging to her damp skin. It was hot and humid summer day and it couldn't be very late in the morning. Kate was a little disoriented because the last thing she remembered was lying with Jordan on the couch. Jordan must have moved her from the couch to their bed sometime through the night, wow, sometimes she could sleep like the dead.

The curtains swayed from the breeze of the opened window. It felt good on her hot skin but it didn't last nearly long enough to cool Kate from the heat of the day. It was going to be a hot one today. Kate loved this time of year. She loved the heat, and cooling off in the lake was so refreshing. She loved the brilliant colours of summer and the smell of fresh cut grass. Something about it just brought her back in time to when she was small and carefree. Kate looked over at the time and saw that it was past nine am, which meant

Jordan had already left for work. Kate frowned she hated that she didn't wake when he kissed her good-bye. Kate knew he had kissed her. Jordan always did. She smiled at the thought of his lips on her skin. She sat back and remembered her night with Jordan. He made her feel so loved and beautiful. Kate smiled and rose from the bed holding onto that happy feeling.

The sheets all fell away and Kate sluggishly walked to the bathroom. The heat made the room so heavy that it was as if her body was weighted down. She rested on the sink and looked in the mirror. Her face was puffy and her hair a curly mess. The humidity made it frizzy and frankly she was a fright to look at. The workout from last night did not exactly help her appearance this morning but she didn't care, she would wake up looking like this every day as long as she woke up feeling happy.

"You are one lucky girl. He is more than you deserve," Kate told her reflection.

Then she padded off to a hot shower. The shower felt good and refreshing, stepping out into the air didn't feel quite as bad as it had. Kate dressed in a light t-shirt and cotton shorts, threw up her hair very long hair into a pony tail. It didn't matter how she wore it, the curls in her hair bounced up and poofed right out. Kate preferred to wear her hair down. She liked the crazy way it fell. It made her feel wild and free, but it was way too hot to have that much insulation on her neck. She grabbed her purse, pulling out her chap stick, which was the only "make-up" Kate wore and applied it liberally. Smacking her lips, she headed to the kitchen for coffee.

Kate's inheritance was so substantial that she didn't have to pursue a career. Kate had gone to university and studied

Psychology but never did anything with it. She felt like she needed to help people and so she started volunteering in her community.

Of course, it started at the hospital helping to cheer up sick kids in the children's ward, which remained her very favourite project. One day she met a very charming old man, Ronnie, while she was having lunch in the hospital cafeteria. The tables were all taken. Kate was sitting at a table all by herself. She saw the man looking around for a place to sit so she waved him over to sit with her. He thanked her and sat down.

The two got to talking and Ronnie told Kate story after story about his life. Once they were done eating he thanked Kate again, not for sharing her table but for listening to an old man's tales. Ronnie said that he didn't really have anyone who would sit and let him tell his stories or if they did they weren't really paying attention. It made him feel good to have someone interested in what he had to say for once.

That really struck a chord with Kate, she felt like that was sad and wrong. She really enjoyed his stories and she was sure there were other seniors who were neglected just like this old man. Kate recalled during one of Ronnie's stories that he had mentioned he lived in a retirement home.

"Ronnie," Kate called out after him, "where is it that you live?" Kate asked.

"I live in at Stewart Manor," he replied, "Going to catch the bus and head home right now."

"I would be happy to give you a lift. The manor is on my way home," Kate told Ronnie.

It wasn't true but she wanted to do something nice for him. Ronnie nodded. He and Kate walked out to her car and she drove him home. Kate walked him inside and said her good-byes. A nurse walked up and thanked her for brining Ronnie home. Kate asked the nurse about volunteering with some of the senior residents and the nurse pointed her to administration. Before long Kate had added visiting the manor once a week to her list of community involvements.

Finally, Kate spent one day a week helping the local animal care shelter for wounded and abandoned animals. It wasn't an easy job like making children smile or listening to an old man tell her how he caught the biggest fish. It was physically demanding work but Kate loved it. Sure, she got to pet the cats, scratch dog's bellies and feed baby rabbits. She also had to clean dirty kennels, walk untrained dogs, and lift large buckets of feed. The shelter was just as rewarding as any other volunteering she did.

Kate liked to take one day during the week to be alone. It was her day to sleep in late, laze around the house and read a book, or go outside for a walk. Kate liked the time to reflect on her week and plan for the next one.

Today was Kate's "me day". She headed into Jordan's home office, with her coffee, to sit with a book. The maid Lily, who Kate also liked to call a friend, would often leave a new book that she thought Kate might like to read. Kate had finished a book and was ready for a new one. Kate headed over to her favorite chair. It was a large, over-stuffed red lounge chair that she would sink right into and disappear for hours. There on the table by the chair sat a new novel, courtesy of Lily. Kate picked up the novel and read the tittle. Then she checked the back of the book jacket. The novel seemed quite interesting so Kate got comfy and cracked the spine. She was completely engrossed with the characters of the book and time stood still. Kate was finally lifted from her suspended state when she realized how hungry she was.

Kate looked at the clock on Jordan's desk. It read just after two. No wonder she was hungry. She put the book back on the table and headed for the kitchen. She went to the fridge to see if there was something leftover from another night. Kate was in luck and found some left over skillet. She heated it in the microwave, gazing out the window while she waited. It was beautiful outside so Kate ate quickly and headed out for an afternoon walk.

Kate loved the neighbourhood they lived in, the scenery was lush and green, with well-kept lawns and extravagant flower beds. She could smell their fragrances in the softly blowing air. The homes did not sit on top of each other like some neighbourhoods in town. The homes were not new. They all had the charm of another time.

Kate wasn't a gym goer but liked to stay fit, so she walked every day. She could walk for hours and just get lost in the scenery and thought. She really loved to be outdoors with Jordan and their friends. She wished that would happen more often than it did but schedules often didn't fall in line.

Kate finished her walk and headed back to the house. Their place was a cottage frame bungalow, with a stone walkway to the front door and a matching driveway that lead to a two-car garage. The lawn was covered with tall maple and oak trees, each sporting its own flower bed. It was a good thing Jordan had a gardener to maintain the flowers because they would have never made it if Kate was in charge. Kate's mom was a very avid gardener, but that trait was not passed down. Even fake plants didn't stand a chance.

Kate headed into the house and back to the kitchen to see what she would make for dinner. Now, cooking dinner was something she did love to do. Kate loved cooking for Jordan and he was always up to the challenge of being her guinea pig and good or bad he always had a compliment. They rarely went out to eat, and agreed that being home with each other was so much more relaxing then going out to a restaurant.

Kate rustled around in the fridge and freezer before she decided what she was going to make for dinner and then started preparing pots, and the outdoor grill. She busied herself with cooking and cleaning, waiting for Jordan to come home. Finally, everything was ready and it smelled delicious Kate could hardly wait to sit down for dinner. Jordan wasn't home yet so she put it in the warming oven to keep until he was. Jordan ran late sometimes but he usually called if he'd be really late. She waved off her concerns and returned to the office to sit with her book.

Kate struggled to get through her chapter and finally put it aside. She walked over to the window to look outside and watch for Jordan to pull up. It was so not like him to not call. Kate decided to give him a call. Jordan may have been rushed and just wanted to get home so she went over to the desk and dialled his cell number. It rang and rang until his voicemail picked up.

"Hey, baby I was just checking in, it's getting late and I haven't heard from you. I love you," Kate said and hung up the phone after completing her message.

She began to pace between the door and the window, looking out the window every time she approached. After two hours and ten phone calls to his cell, she went into the kitchen and turned off the food. It had dried out and looked awful.

Kate was no longer hungry for it anyway. She went into the living room to put on a show to take her mind off things. She sat not really watching what was playing, she just tuned out the TV. Her mind was going a mile a minute, about any, and all scenarios as to why Jordan was not home.

Kate was in her head so much that hearing the shrill ring of the house phone made her jump. She jumped off the couch and ran for the phone thinking it must be Jordan.

"Hello," Kate said into the receiver.

"Ms. Kate Black?" the caller asked.

"Yes," Kate replied.

"Ms. Black, this is nurse Ruby calling from Victoria General Hospital," said the nurse.

Kate thought how weird it was that the hospital was calling her? She wasn't supposed to be volunteering today. Maybe it was a fundraising campaign.

"Yes, nurse Ruby, how can I help you?" Kate asked.

"Ms. Black, there was a car accident this evening and Mr. Best's car was involved," said the nurse.

Kate's heart was pounding in her chest, "Oh?" Kate said unable to say anything more. She felt like her body switched to auto pilot.

"He was severely injured and is currently in surgery. Mr. Best had you listed as his next of kin," the nurse paused, "The doctors may need you to make some decisions about his medical care."

Kate just stood there paralyzed, accident… Severely injured…. In surgery…. Her love, her whole life was fighting for his life. She was numb, she couldn't move, she couldn't breathe and began gasping for air.

The nurse heard her struggling to breathe, "Just try to breathe slowly Ms. Black. I know this is a shock and you're scared but the best thing to do is to remain calm and get over to the hospital. Mr. Best needs you to be strong."

The nurse was right. Kate knew she had to be strong, but she couldn't find the strength to do it. Tears began to blur her vision, "My parents….", Kate breathed, "My parents were killed," Kate informed the nurse.

"I'm sorry to hear that Ms. Black, and this must be very difficult for you, but you found the strength to make it through that and I'm sorry that you need to, but you need to find that strength again. You will make it through this," the nurse said trying to be reassuring.

Kate winced, what strength did she find? She was a wreck that day and she was wreck now. After a few minutes, Kate's breathing slowed and she stood, her legs were strong under her which surprised her. Kate's brain finally kicked in and she dropped the phone. Rushing to grab her purse from the kitchen she headed as fast as she could to the hospital. Leaving the phone hanging off the desk and the nurse calling out, "Ms. Black are you still there?"

Chapter 6

Jordan sat back in his office chair gazing out the window. The sky was light blue with a few white clouds moving lazily along. The sun was shining through his tenth story office window. Although the office was cooled by air conditioning, Jordan could feel the heat of the sun and longed to be outside. His office felt confined and stuffy. Jordan would give anything to be able to open a window and let the fresh air blow in, but not one window opened. Kate always had a window open at home letting the fresh air in. It always smelled like sunshine when he was at home. Jordan longed for the smell of sunshine and he longed for Kate.

Ahh… Kate, Jordan thought to himself. His beautiful, amazing, generous, loving girlfriend. He hoped that would soon change. Jordan had been carrying a solitaire diamond ring around for weeks waiting for the right time to propose to Kate. He would get so close to asking her and then he would chicken out. He wanted to propose so badly but he feared Kate's answer. They hadn't really talked about marriage and Kate never really offered any insight into her thoughts on it. Jordan tried a number of times to bring up the topic of marriage but every time the subject came up, a change of topic occurred, leaving Jordan to wonder if she was purposefully ducking the topic.

Jordan knew he wanted to marry Kate. She had made him happier than he ever thought possible. He decided, win or lose, he was going to ask her. So, Jordan bought the perfect ring and put it in his pocket, there it has stayed, aside from the few times he pulled it out to torment himself with it.

Chicken, Jordan thought to himself. He should have done it last night. The music was playing and they were dancing, wrapped in each other's arms. Their hearts were so in sync, he should have dropped to one knee then. He let the moment pass and the night, although perfect and passionate, did not lead to a marriage proposal.

That's it! Tonight! Tonight, is the night. Jordan decided he would ask Kate to be his wife. He smiled remembering how he left her this morning. Kate was sleeping so deeply, her brown curly hair a mess, taking over the pillow. She had a small smile on her face. He hoped she was dreaming of him. Jordan had leaned over her and kissed her cheek before he left for work this morning and she reached out and stroked his face.

"Have a good day my love," she said more to the air than to him.

Jordan chuckled. Even dead to the world Kate responded to his touch and that was very appealing. It took all of Jordan's will power to walk out of the bedroom and leave for work.

Jordan loved touching Kate's soft skin, making her shudder with pleasure. Darn it, now all he could think about was touching her again, making love to her like he did last night.

Jordan replayed the night's passion over and over in his mind, making him smile every time.

They were both so spent after, that they fell asleep with Kate lying on top of him. Jordan had woken to the darkness, Kate still laying on him. He maneuvered around until he had Kate in his arms. Jordan stood lifting Kate. She wrapped her arms around his neck and nuzzled into his chest. Jordan laid her on their bed and covered her with the comforter. Kate rarely slept under the covers. She tossed herself about until she managed to get her leg out from underneath along with her butt cheek.

It made Jordan smile, thinking of Kate lying there one cheek out and her hair in disarray. Darn it! He was back to wanting her, making it quite difficult to stay in his seat and not drop everything so he could throw her to the bed and have his way with her. Easy tiger, Jordan thought to himself, there is life outside those bedroom walls, but why, why did there have to be?

Jordan forced himself to return to his work, pushing papers and taking phone calls until it was quitting time. He looked at the time it was close enough to five that he was ready to throw in the towel for the day. Jordan gathered his keys and wallet from the top drawer of his desk and he headed out the door. He made his way through the maze of offices and emerged into the lobby. He waived to the secretary.

"I'm done for the day," Jordan called, "if anybody needs me, tell them don't! Because I am not available."

"Yes, Mr. Best, have a nice night," replied Nancy, his secretary of now ten years. Nancy was good at her job and knew him well. She could anticipate what he needed or wanted before he even asked. Nancy was getting close to retirement. She was nearing her sixties. Jordan would have to find another Nancy. An impossible task.

Jordan turned around walking backwards, "You too Nancy, please say hi to Harry for me," he replied.

Nancy took pride in her appearance and always looked professional. She had a classic look which suited her perfectly. She wore her brown hair in a short bob, that complimented her thin frame. Her eyes were a dull green and she wore very little make up, and even that wasn't necessary. She must have been a heart breaker when she was younger and on the prowl. She probably had to beat the girls off with a stick. Nancy was married to a very lovely woman named Harriett, who preferred to go by Harry.

Jordan turned back around and headed to the elevator, stepping in as he pushed the button for the first floor and waited for the descent to be completed. The doors opened with a ding and he was off to find his car parked in his reserved spot just outside the front doors.

Jordan jumped into the car and headed to his favourite florist to pick up a bouquet of flowers. It was a cute little shop about four blocks away. Jordan believed in supporting the local commerce so he tried not to shop at any large chain stores.

He parked out front of the shop and headed in, the door chimed as he walked in causing the woman behind the counter to look up. Jordan looked around for a little bit, not quite sure what he wanted to get. Kate did not have a favorite flower. She just loved getting them and he loved how happy she looked when he handed her an arrangement.

After a few minutes the woman behind the counter joined him.

"Mr. Best, it's very nice to see you. How can I help you today?" she asked.

"Carol, you look lovey today. I see you got some sun!" Jordan replied.

Carol blushed, "I did. A few friends and I went out to the island for a few days, the weather was perfect," she told him.

"That sounds like fun. Listen, I am looking for a flower arrangement, something over the top. I want it to say, big night!" Jordan told Carol waving his hands through the air for exaggeration.

"How much are you looking to spend?" She asked Jordan.

"There is no price point for this night," Jordan responded to Carol.

Carol took Jordan through the different options she could put together. After a few minutes, they had a plan and Carol was off to put it together.

Carol came back with a bouquet of roses in all colours, a few calla lilies sprouted from the center and the whole thing was wrapped in baby's breath. It was perfect. Jordan paid for the flowers and headed back out to his car.

He placed the arrangement carefully in the back seat and began his drive home. His drive was usually very peaceful. Usually the traffic flowed nicely. That was not the case today. Today there was an accident in front of him and it was causing traffic to back up through three intersections. There was no way around it that would lead him home, so, Jordan was stuck waiting to for it to clear up. He was still a little early getting home so he didn't worry about calling Kate to let her know he was stuck in traffic.

Jordan waited patiently. He could see the police and tow truck working diligently to clear the road. Jordan sat watching the street lights turn red, then to green, and then back to red again. He decided to switch on the radio to a local station. It was playing the top ten requested songs. He sat back and enjoyed the music and let the outside noise fade away. Jordan slowly crawled through the traffic jam and after an hour was finally to the last set of lights. He was relieved he would finally be through and on his way home.

Jordan thought maybe he should call Kate and let her know that he was a bit behind but at this point he was about to be set free from the traffic jam and would be home shortly. She was probably in the middle of putting something together for dinner anyway.

Jordan waited for his light to turn green. Once it did he advanced into the intersection. Jordan was unaware of the truck that had ignored the red light and was barrelling toward him. When Jordan did see the truck, it was too late.

In that moment, time was suspended. The front grill of the barreling truck was pushing its way into Jordan's car, the sun reflecting off the metal made it gleam. The shock of the impact seemed to happen too long after the truck collided with his car. Glass from his door shattered and flew in every direction. Jordan put his hands up to shield his face.

The air bags exploded spraying white dust into the air. He felt the bag hit his body slamming him back into the seat. The powder getting into his eyes, causing them to burn.

Jordan felt his car moving sideways and he looked out the passenger side window, only to see the cement base of a street lamp. This was not going to be good, he thought. Jordan prepared for the impact of the cement which came right on cue. Jordan took one last look out the driver's side door to the driver of the truck who had a look of sheer terror on his face, a look Jordan probably reciprocated. Jordan's body slammed back into the truck, his head colliding with the metal grill.

His head only hurt for a few seconds before Jordan realized that he was about to lose consciousness. Jordan was unsure as to whether he was going to make it out of this accident alive and losing control keeping himself conscious, Jordan said a little prayer. Jordan could feel the darkness taking over and just before it went black he thought about Kate. He didn't want to leave her. He wanted a lifetime with her. All he could think was, please God, Kate...

That was his final thought. Then the darkness took him.

Chapter 7

$\mathcal{K}$ate sped through the streets trying to get to Jordan as
fast as possible. She was lucky there were no police cars
on her way. Kate pulled into the hospital parking lot and
parked. She jumped out of the car, barely getting it into park,
and was sprinting across the lot to the emergency room doors.

Once inside she rushed to the nurse's station to get some
information on Jordan's condition. Kate saw a nurse behind
the desk in blue scrubs. She was sitting behind a shield of
glass. Kate was so focused on the nurse and the information
she held that when a hand grabbed her by the arm it made
her jump.

"Hi, Kate. I was here when they brought him in. This is
crazy, I still can't believe it," Kate recognized the voice, it was
Vick.

Vick was the younger brother of Jordan's best friend Todd.
They all grew up together in the same private school. That was

until Jordan left school and was tutored from home so that he could take the helm of his parents' business. However, their bond remained inseparable.

Then Kate came along. Kate and Todd were instant friends, having many of the same interests. Kate and Vick never really managed to get their relationship off the ground. They were not very good friends, if you could call them friends at all.

"I'm going to stay here until there is news on Jordan. I've called Todd already and he is on his way," Vick informed Kate.

Kate looked at Vick and noticed he was in his scrubs. He must be working tonight she thought.

"Aren't you on duty," Kate asked not sure why she cared. All she wanted to do was talk to the nurse and find out what was going on with Jordan.

"I was, but as soon as I realized it was Jordan, the head nurse relieved me and called in a backup," Vick replied.

Kate nodded and headed to the counter.

"I'm already on it," Vick said making Kate stop, "He is still in surgery, there's been no update from the doctor yet. I swear I'm asking every fifteen minutes," Vick said and waived towards the nurse's station.

The nurse behind the desk gave Vick a look of sympathy and said, "Still no news."

Kate thought maybe it could be good to have Vick here, she was sure if she asked the nurse every fifteen minutes they might get annoyed with her. Vick headed to the double doors and swiped his key card, letting them both in. He directed her down one hall and then another until they reached a room, the sign reading "Waiting Room for Families of Surgical Patients Only". Vick opened the door and then went in to sit down.

Kate followed Vick in and sat down. Kate sat for a while and then got up and paced the room. She repeated that pattern only being interrupted by Vick leaving in search of an update. Kate peered out the small window of the door to watch Vick as he questioned a nurse at the closest desk.

It was almost 9:30 before any news came. Jordan had been in surgery since about six o-clock. Vick had gone out for another update and Kate could tell there was something wrong because Vick lowered his head after the nurse spoke. Kate's heart began to race as she watched Vick walked slowly back to the waiting room.

"What is it? What's wrong?" Kate asked frantically.

"One of the surgical nurses called down and said that it's going to be a while yet. They ran into some complications, but his heart rate and blood pressure remain steady," Vick informed Kate.

"Steady? What does that mean? And what complications?" Kate asked Vick hysterically.

"It means that his heart hasn't stopped on the table, and I don't know what complications, they won't tell me that," Vick snapped.

"Oh no, his heart could stop?" This was bad, very bad, Kate sank into her seat tears brimming her eyes, "Will they tell me what complications?" Kate asked.

"Yes, the Doctor will when he gives you a full update," Vick responded.

"So, we wait?" Kate said quietly.

"Yep," Vick acknowledged.

It was after eleven pm when Todd finally walked into the room. Kate knew Vick was texting Todd after every update check. Vick had informed Kate that Todd was out of town on business but was driving back as fast as he could.

Todd and Jordan might technically be friends but when it really came down to it they were truly brothers. Kate saw Todd rushing towards them and flew into the waiting room. He gave Vick a quick hug and then sat beside Kate. Without saying a word, Todd wrapped his big burly arms around Kate and squeezed. Kate had been strong and managed to hold herself together, but that one hug was all it took and Kate's tears were flowing like an open faucet.

Todd held Kate while she cried. Todd was crying too. She could feel his tears hitting her on the shoulder. It was hard for Kate to know that Todd was just as scared as she was. Vick didn't show any emotion he just paced back and forth until the doctor finally came into the room. They all sprang to their feet anxious to know the condition of the man they all loved.

"Ms. Black," the Doctor spoke directly to her, "Would you like to discuss this alone?" he asked looking at Todd and Vick.

Kate shook her head no, "They're family please go ahead."

"Alright," the doctor said clearing his throat and began a detailed summary of what Jordan's injuries were, what they did in surgery and the complications that occurred. It turned out that Jordan's heart did stop and they had to use the shock paddles to revive him twice near the end of the surgery.

As the doctor spoke Kate's legs began to get very weak. She slowly returned to her seat while listening to the doctor's words.

"He is in intensive care unit under heavy sedation and will remain that way until the swelling goes down. Which could be a couple of days or a couple of weeks, I just can't say. Right now, it's up to Jordan's body to heal. Now given the extent of the surgery there may be further complications, such as his heart giving out again, Miss Black, as the next of kin we look to you for medical direction. Would you like us to continue to attempt resuscitation or would you like to sign a document that tells us not to make any efforts to revive him? Please keep in mind that at this point we have no idea if there is brain damage or not," the doctor said.

This whole conversation felt like it was happening to someone else. Kate thought, I can just go home and Jordan would be there waiting for me. But that was not the reality. The reality was that everyone was looking at her waiting to hear what she wanted to do about Jordan's care.

What would Jordan want? This was too much to have to think about. Kate placed her head in her hands and took a deep breath. Well, Jordan did make her next of kin, so she was going to do what she wanted.

"Continue to make efforts," Kate replied to the Doctor. She heard Vick and Todd both let out the breath they were holding. Of course, Kate wanted Jordan alive and back to his life, back to their life, and if that was selfish then that's just too darn bad.

The doctor nodded and just before he left, he told them that a nurse would bring them up to Jordan's room shortly. So, they waited again. Finally, after what felt like eternity, they were following a heavy-set nurse through the hospital. Kate couldn't think any more about anything, her head hurt so badly. She just followed the nurse watching her butt move side to side with every step. It was so hypnotic that Kate almost walked right into the nurse when she stopped.

The nurse directed them to the room on the right and told them they could only go in two at a time.

"Come on Stacy, it's me," Vick said to the nurse.

The nurse paused and looked at Kate, Todd then back to Vick.

"I only see two visitors and one personnel," said the nurse and she walked away.

"Kate, you go ahead. Vick and I will give you a minute alone," Todd offered.

Kate nodded and pushed the door to Jordan's room open. She could hear the beep and swishes of the machines before she saw him. Kate rounded the corner and saw him laying there, his face swollen, black and blue. Tubes and wires were coming out from every direction of the blanket.

The sight of him made her legs give out from underneath her and she crashed into the garbage can as she hit the floor. The crash was loud and Todd and Vick came running into the room. They saw her on the floor and just as Todd reached her, Kate's stomach rolled over, causing her to vomit. Todd rubbed her back until the heaving subsided. Then Todd wrapped his arms around her and lifted her to her feet, holding her there a little longer than necessary. He probably wanted to be sure that she had her footing, Kate thought. Todd helped her to the chair beside the bed supporting her the entire time. Kate sat and looked at Jordan. All Kate could do was sit there and stare at the man she loved lying unmoving in a hospital bed.

Kate's mind finally cleared from its haze and she pulled her chair right up to the side of Jordan's bed and put the side rail down. Kate took his hand carefully so as, not to disturb the wires, and laid her head on the side of his bed holding his hand to her face.

"Jordan, baby...." Kate whispered, "Please, please don't leave me."

Kate quietly let the tears fall until she was so exhausted from the day that she fell asleep without moving an inch.

Chapter 8

Kate woke to an arm stroking her back. It took a few minutes for her to become fully awake and remember the previous day's events. Once it all came flooding back she sat up with a start thinking it was Jordan's hand on her back, but one glance at Jordan and it was clear it wasn't him. Jordan looked exactly the same as he did last night, only in the light of day was his injuries looked much worse. Kate turned to find the owner of the arm, Todd.

Kate's heart clenched and pain made her double over. She began sobbing uncontrollably, pulling her knees up to her chest.

"Todd, I can't do this. I can't say goodbye to another person I love," Kate said between sobs.

"I know, Kate, but let's try to remain optimistic. Jordan's here and he's a fighter. We won't really know anything until the doctor takes him off sedation," Todd said and knelt down to be at eye level, and lifted her chin, "Have strength and faith that Jordan's coming back to us," he told her.

Kate nodded, "You're right. I'm sorry to be so pathetic and weak. Here I am so consumed with my own grief that I didn't even acknowledge yours. I know Jordan is like a brother to you and here you are putting your own feelings aside to help me," Kate said embarrassed.

Todd smiled softly, placing a hand on her leg. Kate was uncomfortable and she squirmed from his touch. Todd, not aware, looked over at the bed where his friend lay motionless.

"He would want me to be here with you since he can't. Jordan would expect that I take care of what he loves most in this world," he said.

"So, his convertible then?" Kate said, her attempt to lighten the weight that was pressing down on both their shoulders.

Todd chuckled softly, "That too!"

Todd stepped back and leaned against the wall just looking at Jordan, with a far off look in his eyes. Kate could only imagine what was going through his mind.

"Oh, I woke you because the Doc's coming in soon to check him over. Vick told me before he left," Todd informed Kate.

"Vick left?" Kate asked puzzled.

"He went to get coffee and food. I just hope Vick remembers we could use coffee too," Todd replied.

"Oh," was really all Kate could say. She was glad Vick had gone. The room seemed colder when he was in it. Kate never quite understood why Vick disliked her so much but it was very apparent he did. The two tolerated each other for sake of the others.

Todd and Kate sat without speaking a word. the only sounds were of the machines attached to Jordan and the bustle of the people outside the hospital room. It wasn't long before the doctor came in and checked Jordan over. They watched impatiently, waiting for the doctor to speak.

"Well, Jordan made it through the night without any complications, that is promising," the doctor told them.

The doctor went over a bunch of numbers on Jordan's machines trying to explain everything but Kate couldn't concentrate or process the information. The Doctor told them he would check in on Jordan again before the end of his shift.

Todd sighed, "I'm glad the doc's happy."

Kate nodded, and turned back to Jordan.

"I'm going to get us some coffee, I'm going stir crazy and need to burn off some energy. I'll be right back," Todd said as he crossed the room towards the door.

Kate didn't reply, but she was glad to have a moment alone. Kate pushed the chair back over to Jordan's bed and she ran a finger over the side of his face. It was warm. She placed her head to his chest and listened to his heart beat instead of the beep of the machine. It seemed strong and regular. Kate didn't really know why, but hearing it gave her some comfort and hope. She closed her eyes and just listened for a while.

The hours in the hospital turned into days, and the days into weeks. Kate only left the hospital when Todd forced her to. He insisted that she go home to shower, eat and get some sleep in her own bed. If Kate wasn't with Jordan either Todd or Vick was. Jordan had no other family than the three of them. They had other friends and Vick and Todd kept them up to date on Jordan's condition. Kate never saw or talked to anyone but Todd, Vick, and hospital staff. She spoke out loud to Jordan, hoping for a response.

It took about three weeks for the swelling in Jordan's brain to dissipate, which Kate assumed was a very long time. Thankfully there were no other complications from Jordan's injuries allowing the doctor to take Jordan off sedation.

Kate hoped it would be a quick process but soon learned it was another waiting game. The Doctor removed a bag from Jordan's IV stand.

"It will take a few hours for the medicine to wear off, so we will have to wait and see how things go from here," the Doctor told them.

Vick had to work a double shift that day, so, he would pop his head in every couple of hours to see how things were going. Each time Kate could see how disappointed he was to see Jordan still lying in the bed.

By the end of the day the anticipation of Jordan waking diminished and concern began to set in.

"I was hoping he would have woken by now," the doctor said. Kate could see the worry on his face. "I've ordered a few tests to take place tomorrow to get a better idea of what is going on. We should know more then," the Doctor nodded to Kate and walked out of the room.

Tears started to fall. Kate was so disappointed, she was sure they would have Jordan back now. Todd reached over to take her hand.

"He's a fighter," Todd reminded her.

Kate nodded but the words didn't really bring her any comfort. Kate stayed with Jordan that night. The next morning two nurses came in and wheeled Jordan and away. Kate sat in his empty room and waited while the nurses and doctors ran all the tests the doctor had ordered. Jordan was returned to his room after lunch.

Kate was hoping to see the Doctor right away and asked the nurse when he would be in with the results. The nurse informed Kate that the results would probably not be ready until the next day. The nurse told Kate to go home and recharge, which was seconded by Vick. Leaving Vick in Jordan's room, Kate reluctantly went home for a hot shower and a long cry.

Kate returned to the hospital early the next morning, attempting to beat the doctor to Jordan's side. Todd and Vick both had to work so she was on her own this time. She promised to call as soon as she got the results. Kate hadn't been there an hour when the doctor came through the door. He busied himself with checking the machines and marking things in Jordan's chart.

"Is anyone else joining us this morning?" the doctor asked while he worked.

Adrianna Cote

Kate shook her head no, she couldn't speak, she just needed to know what the test results said.

"Well," the Doctor said pausing, "Jordan's injuries are healing up very nicely, and his scarring is not as bad as I thought it would be. His vitals are strong. The results of all the tests are negative aside from his brain function test," the doctor said.

Kate's palms got sweaty and the room started to spin, she bit the inside of her mouth hoping the pain would help her regain her focus.

"The EEG and MRI show very low brain function, but it is measuring some and that's a good sign. Now there can be many reasons for the low functioning. Worst case being brain damage, but more likely it's because Jordan remains in a coma. It could be his body's way of taking care of itself," the doctor said and paused to looked at his chart again.

"I can't say how long Jordan will remain in a coma, that part will be up to him. Now, given Jordan's injuries are well on their way to healing. He has been stable since the surgery. I feel he no longer requires to be in the Intensive Care Unit. I am going to have Jordan transferred to our Long-Term Care Unit, where he will still get the care he needs, and I will continue to monitor him daily," the doctor said pausing again. He took his eyes from the chart and looked to her asking, "Ms. Black do you have any questions for me?"

Kate shook her head no and thanked him. The Doctor gave Kate a nod and moved on to other patients. The move to the new unit did not take long. Jordan was settled into his new room by early afternoon. Kate sat in a chair by the window and looked out over the street.

Kate sat in that chair every day and watched people rushing around, walking their dogs, horns honking. Life goes on, Kate thought, even though hers has been at a standstill for almost two months. It took another two months before Todd had finally convinced Kate to try to return to her daily Life. Vick promised to check in on Jordan throughout his shifts at the hospital and the nurses had her number and promised to call at the slightest change in Jordan's condition. So, Kate agreed to try to get back to her life.

Kate was successful for three whole days. She went to the animal shelter and the senior residence. She even went to the children's' ward with bags of goodies for the kids, but nothing felt the same. Kate didn't get any joy from those things any more. Then came Kate's "Me Day" a day where there were no distractions just Kate sitting with her own thoughts.

The silence of the house was deafening. Kate couldn't recall it ever being so quiet. Kate's thoughts were always about Jordan. Maybe something is wrong and she's not there. Maybe the doctor has some news and she's not there. She fantasized often about Jordan waking up and she was not there. That one terrorized her the most. Kate couldn't just sit in her house reading a book, so she returned to her new daily life and that was at the hospital with Jordan.

Chapter 9

Kate knew everybody was worried about her being at the hospital all day, every day. They wanted her to do other things but she didn't care.

"Jordan would not have wanted you to give up your life and wait for him," Todd said one day while he was visiting.

"I know," was Kate's response trying not to start a fight, but at the same time thinking to herself, how would anybody know what Jordan would want? Did they sit down and talk about it one time over beers?

"Hey, Todd, make sure if I end up in a coma that Kate doesn't sit around the hospital waiting for me to wake up," Jordan would say, Kate thought sarcastically to herself.

All Kate knew was if the roles were reversed Jordan would be by her side.

Time dragged on, it felt like it had been years, but it had only been months since Jordan's accident. The Doctors went from being optimistic about Jordan waking up to being stumped as to why he was not waking. They ran all their tests and could not come up with a single reason why Jordan remained in a coma so they defaulted to the answer that Jordan must have suffered severe brain damage. The days ticked by. The Doctor seemed less and less convinced that Jordan would wake at all. Kate was not ready to believe that.

"Kate, nobody wants to believe Jordan is gone, but we may have to start accepting the fact that he may not wake up," Todd said one afternoon.

"No, I don't believe that, his body is strong. Jordan's heart is beating on its own, he's breathing on his own. He's coming back," Kate replied earnestly.

"The doctor explained that Jordan's body sustaining itself could account for the low brain function," Todd returned.

"Could be. It's unclear, we can't say for sure. So, with all that why would I give up hope?" Kate demanded, it sounded like Todd had already decided Jordan was gone, and she hated that.

"No, do not give up hope, always have hope, but get on with your life," Todd coaxed.

Todd wasn't wrong, but he wasn't right either. So, what was she to do? She wanted to yell out to Jordan for an answer. However, this time, unlike her parent's funeral Kate had a feeling there wasn't going to be a guy about to hand her a white envelope holding words of comfort.

Kate sighed, "I don't know Todd, I just don't know how I'm supposed to do that."

"How about this? Take the weekend and get away, go out to the cottage, think about things, get some distance and perspective and come back fresh and hopefully with an idea as to what to do next," Todd suggested.

"The cottage?" Kate questioned him with scrutiny, "How would that give me perspective, I would see Jordan everywhere," she finished.

"OK, fair enough then another property. Jordan has many holdings, find one you guys haven't been to," Todd suggested.

Vick walked in just as Todd was speaking, "Couldn't help but overhear, Jordan has a great place in Northern Ontario, man, what was it called Nobishing? No, Missisping, no that's not it. Nosbonsing! It's a lake, in a town just outside of," Vick paused in thought, "North Bay! It's a nice town, very peaceful," Vick offered.

"Andrew would know where it is," offered Todd.

Andrew was Jordan's attorney. He had taken over Jordan's affairs after her father had passed. Andrew was good at his job and very professional but lacked her father's familiar nature. Andrew was not the type to mix business and pleasure.

"I don't know, leaving Jordan an entire weekend alone?" Kate asked to no one in particular. Was she actually considering this? Leaving Jordan not only for the day but leaving town for a weekend? Kate asked herself.

"Go! Get away from it all, it'll be good for everyone," Vick said sounding very sarcastic.

Kate looked at Vick questionably, did Vick just tell her to get lost? Kate thought to herself. Regardless of Vick's comment, Kate was hesitant and they all knew it.

"What if we promised to sit by Jordan's side on your behalf the entire time you were gone?" offered Todd. "We would call you at the slightest twitch."

"Seriously?" Vick asked Todd.

Todd gave Vick a stern look.

"Fine," Vick huffed. "I'm off Saturday so I can relieve you Friday at two pm when I'm done work and stay until Sunday morning at six o'clock," he said shrugging off Todd's stare.

Todd smiled, "I can take over on Sunday and I can also do Monday Morning, I don't have any meetings until three thirty that afternoon. That way you can travel up Friday and have two solid days there and travel back Monday," Todd said using his "I'm in charge" tone.

Todd was used to telling his assistants what to do and sometimes forgot he wasn't talking to them but to his friends. Kate chuckled. Jordan would get so irritated with Todd when he did that.

"Yes, Boss," Kate replied, which would have been Jordan's retort.

Todd blushed slightly, softly chuckling too, "Sorry, its automatic."

Vick clapped his hands together and said, "Well now that that's hashed out I'm leaving."

He gave Jordan a quick pat on the arm and headed out of the room.

"Do you want me to call Andrew about the cabin?" asked Todd.

"No, I'll call him this afternoon," Kate replied.

Kate still wasn't sure she was going to go but she didn't want to say that to Todd. They were both pretty stubborn and could have been at it for a while. Kate just wanted to be alone with Jordan.

Todd nodded and with one more glance at his best friend still lying in a hospital bed and a longing glance at Kate, he turned and left.

Alone again with her thoughts, Kate continued to debate whether she was going or staying. Suddenly, her body was full of nervous energy, so she stood to pace the room. Kate ranted to the air about the pro and cons of this trip and at times offering a response as if it were from Jordan. After about an hour Kate headed down to the cafeteria to get a bite to eat.

Kate rarely ate in the cafeteria but today she needed to have a moment away from the beeping machines to clear her thoughts and decide what she was going to do. Once she was done eating she returned to Jordan's room she picked up her cell and dialled Andrew's office number. Maybe the cottage wasn't available. That would solve that problem.

The secretary picked up after one ring, "Andrew Breli's office, Barb speaking," said the voice on the other line.

"Hi, Barb, its Kate Black calling for Andrew, is he available?" Kate asked.

"I am sorry Ms. Black he is with a client, is there something I can help you with or a message and I will have him return your call at his earliest convenience?" asked Barb.

Kate explained to Barb about Jordan's property in Northern Ontario. She asked if it was available this weekend and how she would go about getting the address and keys. Barb did not have the answers so she told Kate that she would call back as soon as she could speak with Andrew.

Kate hung up the phone, thinking Jordan probably didn't even have that property anymore. She felt that she was wasting both Barb's and her own time looking into it.

Kate's phone rang about forty-five minutes later. Barb had spoken with Andrew and had gotten all the information Kate had asked for. There was a cottage and it was in a little town called Astorville. The cottage was available, because it was not a property Jordan rented out, so Kate could use it whenever she liked.

"There is a property manager taking care of the property. I have requested that he go to the cabin and leave the door unlocked and the keys on the counter. Just leave the keys on the counter and lock up when you leave. The property manager will collect them sometime next week. Have a nice weekend Ms. Black," Barb said and disconnected the call before Kate could tell her she wasn't sure she was going.

Kate continued to go back and forth whether she was going to Astorville or not. The battle continued for the remainder of the day, she even debated it in her sleep that night. She dreamt she was looking in a mirror and her reflection was telling her to go but she was telling her reflection she didn't want to. She woke Friday morning stiff and tired from sleeping on the couch, but had finally decided she would go to the cottage.

Kate packed what she thought she might need for the trip and loaded it into her car. Jordan would usually have Lily pack, so Kate hoped she got everything she would need. Kate made her way to the hospital to sit with Jordan. It's funny how time moves slowly when you want it to hurry up and quickly when you want it to slow down. Time passed so fast that before Kate knew it Vick was walking into the room and pushing her out the door.

"Time to go," Vick said, pulling her from the chair.

Kate went over to the bed and gazed at Jordan like she wasn't going to see him for months. He looked like he was just sleeping peacefully and would wake at any moment. She sighed wishing that were true. Kate leaned her forehead on Jordan's and closed her eyes, then she kissed him.

Kate looked at Vick who had already settled into the chair and was reading a novel. He looked up from his book.

"What are you waiting for? Go!" he commanded.

Man, Vick was such a jerk sometimes. Kate headed to the door, taking one last look at Jordan before she walked out the room. Her chest felt heavy and her eyes began to tear. Kate almost turned around, but she willed herself forward.

Kate had managed to get into her car and was driving. She was minutes from hitting the highway, and if she turned around she was only minutes from Jordan. Drive on. Kate thought to herself. This could be good.

It was a six-hour drive to where she was going, so Kate hit the gas station outside of town, filled up her car with gas, grabbed a couple of energy drinks and snacks. She pulled back out onto the highway, turned up the radio and was on her way.

Chapter 10

The bigger cities quickly became concrete pillars reflected in Kate's review mirror. The number of cars on the road became less and less, until Kate was driving a small four-lane divided highway virtually alone. The scenery came to life with green trees and blue sky unobstructed by high-rises, buildings or stacks spewing smoke. The farther north she got the more wildlife she saw. A fox darted out on to the road, Kate drove by a skunk that didn't make it across the highway, and saw a porcupine waddling into the bush. She was told, by Todd, there were deer, moose and bear up this way and to be careful. Kate hoped she would get to see them, at a distance of course.

It was shortly after seven when Kate found the turn off to the cabin. Her GPS started going haywire, it didn't seem to like this rural area. She turned it off and pulled out the direction Barb had emailed her. Kate followed the notes down one winding road after another until she was finally pulling into the drive of the cabin.

The cabin was not what Kate was expecting of one of Jordan's properties. It was a small rustic cabin with old wood shaker siding. The front had only the door and one window which sported a very full and colourful flower box. It was charming but small. She headed into the cabin with her bags to settle in.

The inside looked just as small as the outside. There was a small bathroom which held a toilet, small sink and a stand-up shower. There was a small bedroom that had a double bed and antique dresser. The closet was used as a linen closet. Although the room was small it was bright due to the floor to ceiling windows that overlooked the lake. The property manager had opened a few of the windows and there was a small breeze coming in off the lake. It smelt like heaven. Finally, there was what Kate would call the great room. It was an open concept living room and eat-in kitchen. This room also had the floor to ceiling windows, however these ones sported French doors.

The French doors led out to a very large deck that had a seating and dining area. The deck was covered with a glass roof and was completely screened in. Just off the deck was a long descending staircase that led to a large dock floating on the water. The floating dock was accompanied by a speed boat. Kate was unsure if the boat was Jordan's or if the property owner just parked his there for the summer. Not that it mattered. Kate wouldn't know how to drive it anyway. Near the end of the dock sat two Muskoka chairs, one red and one white. She decided that would be the perfect spot to start her weekend so Kate headed down the stairs and sat in the white chair.

Vick was right, it was very peaceful, the only traffic was on the lake. There were people out boating and fishing. Kids were jumping off their dock's as parents sat and watched. Kate leaned back letting the sun warm her face, feeling the breeze sweep across it every once in a while. She tried to imagine Jordan in this place and, as small as it was, she could see this being somewhere he would go to be alone.

Kate sat like that until the bugs started to come out to dine. Kate being dinner. She realized she did not bring sunscreen or bug spray, and figured there probably wasn't any food in the kitchen either. She headed inside to check and found she was right. So, Kate checked the map on her phone and drove to the nearest town to get some dinner and do some shopping.

The drive in was easier then she thought, and once she realized she knew where she was going, Kate turned on the local radio station. The radio personality called himself Frankie and was announcing the Psychic Fair at the Farmer's Market the next day. Kate never was one for Psychic nonsense so she turned off the radio and drove the rest of the way in silence.

It was late by the time she got to town and realized that almost all the stores in this town closed at nine, so her options were limited to a department store that was open late and a twenty-four-hour grocery store. Kate went to the department store first grabbing a few items, bug spray, sunscreen and baseball hat. Then she headed to the grocery store and picked up what she thought she might need for the weekend. On her way out, she saw a poster for the Psychic Fair the radio announcer had mentioned. Kate spent a few minutes reading the poster but then waved it off and headed to load the groceries into her car.

It was about ten thirty at this point and Kate wasn't quite ready to head back to the cabin so she drove around the town to see what it was all about. She found its downtown. It was cute with its interlocking stone roadway and old style brick buildings and it looked well kept. Kate drove by what she thought was the Farmers Market, which appeared to be an old train station. It was very charming. She also found a winding street that had a lake on one side and what looked to be a bike or walking path on the other.

The town seemed to shut down at night because Kate rarely met another vehicle on the road. She traveled through a business section of town, where she found a fast food place still open. Kate went through the drive through and ordered a very late dinner. She scarfed it down in the parking lot and headed back out onto the street. As Kate drove the businesses were replaced by houses and open fields, until she hit the end of the road. Fortunately, the end of the road led right back onto the highway Kate needed to get herself back to the cabin. She took that as a sign and jumped onto the highway and headed to her weekend home.

Once at home, Kate unloaded the bags from her car as quickly as she could because the mosquitos had built a wall in front of her and she had to break through every time she went out to her car. Frantically, Kate closed the door after her last trip out to the car, trying to keep out as many bugs as she could. Kate got to work putting away the food. It was midnight before she decided to shower and get into bed.

The window was still opened and the night breeze cooled the room, so Kate snuggled under the warmth of the blankets and closed her eyes. She had a difficult time falling asleep, not because her mind wouldn't shut off but, because she realized she had been inflicted with many bug bites. They were now getting very itchy and there was a mosquito buzzing around her head trying to come in for a landing, Kate swatted blindly trying to get it with one hand and scratched her bug bites with the other.

"Darn it!" Kate said to herself out loud frustrated. She finally became so tired that the irritation from the bug bites dulled until it was completely gone, and sleep took over.

Despite the bug bites, she slept better then she had in months. She woke feeling rested and ready for the day. However, the weather was not cooperating. Outside the window, the sky was grey and overcast. She frowned, but got out of bed and went to the kitchen to make coffee.

She found a radio in the kitchen and turned it on. She tapped her feet to the beat as she waited for the coffee to be ready. Once the machine spit out the last little bit of brown liquid she grabbed a cup, turned up the radio loud and headed out onto the deck to drink her coffee. The air was damp and slightly chilly so she went back in to grab a sweater. Kate got comfortable on one of the outdoor sofas, placed her cup on the table in front of her. She noticed there was a pit of rocks and a knob in front that said "On and Off. So, she turned the knob on and a fire started spewing out from the rocks. Nice! She thought and sat back to enjoy the ambiance of nature and her little fire.

Restless, she decided she couldn't sit all day and headed in to get dressed. The radio announcer spoke about the Farmer's Market downtown. Kate decided since the sun was hiding she would go and check it out. Plus, she needed some itch relief or she was going to scratch the skin right off her body.

She remembered the way to town and maneuvered her way to the market. The only difficult thing was trying to get a parking spot. Apparently, this was a busy little market, and it was a long weekend so tourism was just picking up. Once a space freed up she parked and headed over the village of tents outside the old train station. The wind was still cool and she wondered if it would rain, but didn't care if it did.

She traveled from tent to tent checking out the products. There was homemade jewelry, clothing, fruit and vegetables grown by local farmers. She wished she would have thought of that yesterday and waited to buy her produce here. There were tents that sold baked goods and other concessions selling hot or cold food. Ultimately, she bought some apples from a local farmer and some homemade banana bread from a very nice elderly woman. Near the back of the market was a very large tent that was completely closed-up aside from a small opening. There was a sign outside the tent that read "Psychic and Medium Advisers" Kate had forgotten there was also a physic fair here today. She rolled her eyes and headed into a small tent that had racks of clothing and began to look around, not noticing the women staring back at her.

Chapter 11

Ashley felt her presence right away. It was one of her gifts. Ashley was "gifted" with many talents when it came to the supernatural world, but at times it didn't feel much like a gift. Now was one of those times.

Ashley sensed there was a problem, and then looked up to see a woman entering a merchant tent with the darkest aura she had ever seen. Ashley would have brushed it off, had the very same person not appeared before her as an apparition

"Ok, so are you like her long-lost grandmother?" Ashley asked.

"Oh my…. Can you see me?" asked the apparition excitedly.

"Yes, I can see and hear you," sighed Ashley. "So, who are you then?"

"Well," replied the apparition, "technically I am her."

"OK, what? How does that work?" Ashley asked.

"I don't really know, but I do know that I need to warn her," replied the apparition

"About?" Ashley asked.

"That she will die, that those she loves will die," replied the apparition.

"Well, that's not great news, good luck with that," Ashley replied with a wave of her hand and began to walk away.

"AHHHHHHHHHHHHHHH," screeched the apparition.

Ashley slammed her hands over her ears and yelled "stop it!"

"I will not! I will follow you and drive you crazy until the day she dies," yelled the apparition to Ashley.

"Grrrr...." Ashley growled, she could tell this was not going to end well unless she cooperated, "fine, but why me, there is a whole tent of mediums, why can't you leave me be?"

"I tried, they can't see me. I wasn't sure you could until you spoke to me," replied the apparition.

Ashley rolled her eyes. Great! So, it was her own fault this apparition was talking to her.

"Darn it, fine, what is your name and why is your message so dire?"

* * * * * *

Kate didn't find anything she liked so she headed out of the tent and back to her car with the goodies she did buy. She loaded everything into her car and slammed the trunk closed and jumped back because there was a woman standing at her car.

"I am so sorry, I did not mean to scare you," said the girl apologetically.

"My name is Ashley and I am not a medium. Well I am, but I don't usually use my gift unless I am absolutely forced to," Ashley said, looking more to the side when she said the last part then to Kate.

Kate looked at her questionably and thought great, a psychic was out to try to make a buck off her.

"My gift, or should I say gifts allow me to speak to people that have passed on. I can sense damaged auras and see into past lives," Ashley continued. "It's not very often that I meet someone who signals all three of my gifts at once. I wasn't going to approach you but you have someone here who is very persistent."

"Who?" Kate asked before she even realized the words came out of her mouth.

"Well, you, or another you from a past life," Ashley responded.

Kate laughed with a snort, how absurd she thought. "And how much is this going to cost me?" she asked Ashley, tapping her foot impatiently as she waited for a response.

"Well, your charm certainly goes from life to life," she said speaking off to the side again. Kate rolled her eyes again. Then Ashley turned her attention back to Kate and said, "It won't cost you a thing. Like I said, I don't really do this kind of thing."

Kate was taken back for a minute, then it dawned on her. She'll get a free reading and then she will try to con her into buying some crazy voodoo stuff. But the jokes on her. She wasn't ready to head back to the cabin so she would take the free reading, for all she knew it could be entertaining, but Kate wasn't buying what she was selling.

"Okay so how does this work then?" Kate asked.

"Well we could stand here and talk or we could find a more private spot," Ashley said and nodded to a spot on the green lawn where there was no one around.

Kate nodded and followed across the parking lot to a spot that had very green and lush grass. Kate sat beside Ashely, a little curious about what would come out of Ashley's mouth, she never really had a reading done before.

The two settled under a large maple tree and Kate tucked her knees under her chin and looked at Ashley.

"Just let me get centered and focused on you," Ashley requested, and closed her eyes.

Kate rolled her eyes, at how bogus the whole thing was.

"I saw that!" said Ashley her eyes still closed.

Kate sat up straight, shocked, that Ashley saw Kate roll her eyes? How is that possible? Ashley's eyes were closed? Right, Kate thought sarcastically, Ashley saw it with her "third eye."

* * * * * *

Ashley sat focusing on the images that appeared before her. She tuned out all the noise of the outside world and tuned in to the being before her. Once Ashley was connected it was like she was possessed by the deceased, except at the same time she was herself and able to carry on a conversation with the person that had passed on. When the deceased told their story, Ashley could see and feel what they did, which wasn't always a great thing.

Ashley prepared herself for the journey that lay ahead with the spirit, who called herself Katherine. After a few breaths, Ashley told the spirit to show her story. Ashley knew bits and pieces from talking to the apparition but being present for it made it all very clear to Ashley.

Katherine took Ashley's hand and was instantly brought back in time. Ashley stood before a handsome man, who looked at her with love in his eyes, "We will find a way to be together my love," he said to Katherine.

Katherine reached out to touch his face and was pulled into a passionate kiss. She returned his affection with her own.

Katherine was pulled from the kiss by a noise that came from behind her. She turned and looked. She saw one of the regulars stumbling around after a few too many glasses of Ale. Katherine pulled away from the man quickly.

"We cannot be seen, John, Victor can never know," Katherine said in a panic.

"He's very drunk," replied John, and pulled Katherine back into his embrace.

Katherine and John often met behind the old tavern. The tavern was where Katherine would pick up a barrel of whiskey to bring home to Victor. Katherine and John would meet and slip away to an abandoned shack that was secluded in the forest behind the tavern.

"I am tired of waiting Katherine, meet me tonight in the apple grove at three am, we will run, and never look back," John said.

Katherine stilled, she was scared but she was ready too. She nodded, turned away, she lifted her skirt and headed for home, pulling her last barrel of whiskey home to her husband

Katherine opened the front door to her house and walked in quietly.

"There you are," said her husband, Victor, grabbing her around the waist and slamming his lips to hers, He smelt of whiskey and tobacco. "Where have you been, what took you so long?" he growled.

"You know how I can be. I got caught up in my own thoughts and lost all track of time," Katherine responded, wriggling out of his grip.

"Hmp," Victor retorted, "Dinner, woman, I'm starving."

"Of course, dear," Katherine replied.

Katherine busied herself in the kitchen preparing Victor a plate of stew and corn bread.

Victor slammed himself down at the table and began to shovel the stew into his mouth.

"Whiskey, woman!" Victor commanded slapping Katherine on the backside.

Katherine poured him a glass of amber liquid, wondering how many Victor had already had.

Victor was never Katherine's choice for a husband, but she was forced to marry him by her father or be sent to a monastery. Her father, much like her husband, had very little use for women.

Victor was kind in the beginning, so she thought she had traded for a better life. Victor got mean and rough with Katherine as time went on. It was only a few years into her marriage when Katherine met John. Katherine had escaped from the house one day and went to the pond and there she found John standing in her favourite spot.

They engaged in a conversation. Katherine learned that John's family was new in to town and taking over the tavern. They were drawn to each other from the very moment they met and it didn't take long before they were crossing lines.

Victor slammed his hand down on the table snapping Katherine from her thoughts. "Darn it woman, listen to me."

"I'm sorry, dear, what did you say?" Katherine responded.

"Answer the door," Victor yelled, "Oh! forget it, I'll do it!" he mumbled under his breath.

Victor stumbled to the door and yanked it open, "Franklin!" he called out, "Great to see you, come in! I'll get you some whiskey fresh from the tavern."

"Thank you, Victor, but no, I've come to share some news, if you could step outside, it's not for gentle ears," Thomas requested, meaning Katherine could not hear.

Victor stepped out and slammed the door. Katherine could hear the murmuring of voices and then heard Victor yell and slam something hard against the house. Katherine jumped wondering what could have angered him? She worried about what that meant for her.

After a few minutes, Victor returned to his seat. He was angry, his eyes following her as she moved about the small house. Katherine became afraid that this night would end with her lying on the floor and hiding in the house until the bruises faded away.

Katherine decided it would be better if she readied for bed and headed for the bedroom, but as she passed Victor he grabbed her by the wrist and yanked Katherine down to his lap, holding her there tight.

"Who would have thought you'd turn out to be a jezebel?" Victor asked rhetorically, "I'm thinking we could start a brothel. I'll be the master."

"What?" Katherine asked surprised.

"Don't act all innocent, wench. Tell me, do you lie down just for him or are there others?" Victor asked in a rage.

Katherine blanched. He knew, but how? Franklin must have been at the tavern. Franklin never cared for Katherine

94

and followed Victor everywhere like a lost little puppy. There was no denying it, Franklin would tell Victor if he saw Katherine with another man.

"You have had too much whiskey, Victor, please let's just go to bed, you're not making any sense," Katherine said hoping Victor would sleep it off, but knowing he wouldn't.

"Woman, I will take you to bed and I will tie you there. I will do as I want with you and then I will sell you to a brothel," Victor said vehemently.

Katherine knew she was in trouble and rather than deny it she began to beg for her life.

"No, Victor, Please, I'm sorry," Katherine begged.

"Shut up!" Victor yelled getting to his feet and throwing her to the floor. He began undoing his belt to release his trousers, "I'm going to tear you in two and then I'm going to pass you around, might as well make a bit of coin for my misery," Victor said as he stumbled and fell into a chair.

Katherine took the opportunity to get to her feet and back into the kitchen. Victor cornered Katherine and tried to grab her. Katherine wasn't thinking and grabbed the closest thing, which was a cast frying pan and hit Victor with it with all her might. He stumbled back and then fell to the floor. Katherine didn't take the time to see if he was alright, she ran out the door and into the woods. Katherine made her way to the apple grove and waited for John to arrive.

It was a cold night and Katherine didn't think to grab a coat as she ran out the door trying to get away from Victor. She pulled herself into a ball trying to keep warm. Finally, John arrived and pulled Katherine into his arms. Katherine began to sob and told him about her escape.

"Your safe now," John said as he held her, "We will never see him again."

John brought his mouth to hers and Katherine welcomed it, and let the warmth wash over her.

John suddenly pulled from the embrace and put his hand to his head with a stunned look on his face. Then Katherine saw him. It was Victor, holding a rock in his hand, standing behind John.

"You're right about that," Victor said. "You'll never see anyone again."

Then Victor brought the rock down hard on John's head again. John's body went limp and hit the ground hard. Katherine fell to her knees screaming and crawled over to John.

"Oh, no, no, no," Katherine cried, "This is all my fault," she sobbed.

"That's right, this is all your fault," Victor said matter of fact, "You sinned Katherine. You sinned against me and you've sinned against God. I swear you will never have the love of a man, I will always take it from you," Victor threatened, his voice getting louder as he spoke.

His rock yielding hand came crashing down on her, and that's when Katherine 's world went black.

When Katherine woke, she felt like she was floating, she looked around and realized she was standing over a woman

Adrianna Cote

lying bloody on the ground. Katherine leaned in to get a closer look and jumped back because she saw herself. Katherine knew in that moment that she was dead. She turned and looked around and saw that she was back in her living room. Victor must have brought her body back to the house.

Victor came into her focus. He was sitting in his chair holding his pistol. Victor was crying and mumbling.

"You made me do it," he sobbed, "I gave you a good life, what more could you have asked for?" Victor asked the body lying at his feet. "I did love you," he whispered.

With those last words, he put the gun to his head and pulled the trigger.

Chapter 12

Ashley and Katherine were jolted back into the present. Ashley's mind was reeling. It took her a moment to gather her thoughts and calm herself, that vision was intense.

"I have spent many lifetimes trying to figure out why I am stuck here. I want to move on but everything I try leaves me more discouraged. It took me a long time to figure out what was going on," Katherine said, "but I did, and as I realized what needed to happen, everything came into focus. It's hard to explain why I think after all these years I finally know what to do, but my conviction is firm," Katherine said.

"And what would that be?" Ashley asked.

"After watching many of my lives pass by, I realized that John, Victor and I are irrevocably, connected lifetime after lifetime. That night's events have us tied together for eternity," Katherine continued. "John and I always find each other, but somehow Victor always ends up getting hurt by our

98

love. Sometimes Victor retaliates in very destructive ways, other times it's fate that steps in but John and I, or the living ones, always end up dying in some violent way and all would be lost, until we were all born again."

"So, what is keeping you here?" Ashley asked.

"It seems my guilt, John's guilt, and Victor's anger over the course of what happened in our lifetime has caused our spirits to separate into two. One half being forced to live and repeat a sequence of events and the other half is forced to watch life play out again, not able to change anything. Year after year, life after life, I am constantly trying to find a way to save the living versions of us, but it is always the same results," Katherine paused.

"I wouldn't care so much if John and I could be together now, but his spirit is held in a prison that I can't free him from. Again, I don't know how things became clear, they just did," said Katherine. "Kate," she said pointing at Kate sitting waiting for Ashley to do her reading, "she can fix this, she just needs to right the wrong done to Victor of her time, because in his own way he does love her. Just like my Victor loved me. You must tell Kate the story, tell her that if she doesn't fix things everyone will die. Again."

Ashely nodded and began the reading with Kate.

* * * * * *

Kate sat there in disbelief. The reading she had gotten from Ashley was nothing like she expected. Kate thought there would be cards or a crystal ball telling her future. All Kate got was this crazy story about some woman named Katherine. That Katherine was linked to Kate cosmically. The good news being that everybody dies, Kate thought sarcastically. This was not entertaining at all.

"So, you're saying that I am being haunted by myself?" Kate asked sarcastically.

"Yes, sort of, you could sum it up that way," Ashley responded.

Kate stood and wiped the grass that was clinging to her legs, "Well, this has been swell. Thanks for that," then Kate turned to walk away.

"Wait!" Ashley called out, jumping to her feet.

Kate stopped and looked back to Ashley. Oh, here we go, Kate thought rolling her eyes. This is where she tries to sell the voodoo bag. Kate turned without a word and waited for Ashley's sales pitch.

"I'm just a middle man and can only give you the information presented to me, what you do with it is entirely up to you. Bit there is one more thing," Ashley said.

"Of course, there is," Kate said under her breath.

"Katherine says the only way to fix things is to right the wrong done to the Victor of your time, because he does love you. She also says that if you need her, or should I say you, the only way to find her is to find her level of....," Ashley paused, "lets call it consciousness," she finished.

"What?" Kate asked absolutely bewildered.

"Kate, Katherine was very adamant that you either fix things or everybody dies, again," Ashley warned.

All Kate could do was nod and then walked away. She was just so perplexed. That was definitely not what she thought was going to happen when she agreed to a free reading.

Finally, after a moment, Kate's mind cleared and she thought to herself, no wonder Ashley doesn't work as a psychic. She is terrible at it.

"What the heck was that?" Kate asked herself aloud as she headed for her car.

She couldn't get enough distance between her and that crazy lady.

* * * * * *

Ashely watched as Kate walked to her car and drove away.

"I don't know Katherine. I don't think she really believed what I was saying," Ashley said to the fading apparition.

"I hope she does because if not," Katherine paused, "they are all going to die," she said sadly and disappeared.

Ashley felt bad for Katherine, it was a tough spot to be in and to not be able to do anything about it. She was glad she tried to help and hoped it would work out, but Ashley had a feeling things were going to get much worse before they would get better.

* * * * * *

On her drive home Kate kept thinking about the absurdity of the whole story. She had to fix the relationship with Victor. She didn't even know a Victor, let alone have one in love with her and what the heck was that whole thing about level of consciousness.

The whole thing was absurd, so absurd that all she could do was laugh. That medium almost got her, Kate thought to herself.

"Ha, she was good after all," Kate said out loud. She probably thinks I'm going to run to her for more information and that's when she is going to charge an arm and a leg, Kate thought.

"Well, the jokes on her, I'm still not buying," Kate announced.

Kate started laughing about the whole ordeal. Before she knew it, she was laughing uncontrollably. First, she was laughing about the crazy medium lady, then she didn't know why she was laughing but she couldn't stop. Kate was laughing so hard she had to pull over to catch her breath and clear the tears from her eyes.

Kate gave that medium one thing. She lifted the tension that had been weighing Kate down for months. She started driving again and realized she felt freer than she had in months.

Kate almost forgot that she needed some itch relief. S decided to the store to grab some on her way out of town. She parked and headed into the store, trying to clear her thoughts of Ashley and Katherine and start thinking about what she was going to do when she got home and back to her life.

As Kate walked she felt lighter, and realized Todd might have been right. Maybe this was exactly what she needed.

Kate didn't like how much Todd was pushing her to move on with her life and at times got very uncomfortable with his presence. Todd stood a little too close, or hugged a little too long. Jordan and Todd were best friends, brothers really, and he would do anything for Jordan and therefore would do anything for Kate.

Kate pushed her feelings aside. She was defiantly reading too much into it. She decided she needed a glass of wine after her eventful afternoon. She grabbed what she needed from the store and headed back to the cabin. Once back at the cabin she poured herself a large glass of red wine and took it out onto the back deck.

The sun had decided to finally poke through, so Kate spent the afternoon on the dock, people watching, until the bugs drove her inside again. Once inside she began to poke around the little cottage and see what there was. Kate wondered how Jordan had acquired this little cottage. She found some old photo albums and began looking through them. It didn't take long before she realized that they were albums of Jordan and his parents when he was just a boy. The little cottage was in the background in a lot of the pictures. So, the cottage was his parent's and a place he could remember them. Kate wondered why Jordan never told her about this place.

Kate understood having a spot that made you feel close to someone, she had that with her parents whenever she went to the community park. They used to spend hours there, hiking and fishing, swimming and having picnics. Kate would go there whenever she needed her parents. Funny, she hadn't been there in a long time. With everything that happened to Jordan, Kate should have gone there, but she needed Jordan more then she needed her parents right now.

Looking at the pictures, Kate realized that Jordan had found a way to move on with his life and yet still keep them with him. Kate had done that with her parents too and now she had to find a way to do that again, and wait until Jordan came back to her.

Todd was right again, Kate needed perspective. She needed space to figure things out. Kate didn't have all the answers but she felt like she might at least have a place to start, and that was back home.

Kate decided to pack up and head for home. She dumped out the rest of the wine, turning out the lights as she left the rooms. She dropped the keys on the counter, with one final look at the special cabin, she got into her car and she drove home. It took all evening and part of the night to get there and she was grateful when she finally pulled into her drive at about two am. Kate decided to get some rest before she went up to see Jordan at the hospital. She wanted to be sure she knew what she was going to do before she shared her new-found insight for the future with her friends.

Chapter 13

Todd had come to sit with Jordan around seven in the morning on Sunday. It was a long time to be in one place. Todd could not understand how Kate could be here for days, he'd only been here one night and he already missed his bed. Todd stood by his promise to be with Jordan so Kate could go away, and so he waited patiently for her to return.

Todd looked over at Jordan and watched his chest rise and fall. It was like he was just sleeping. Todd reminisced about when they were young and innocent, not that they were ever innocent. Todd and Jordan were trouble makers and terrorized their school. That is until Jordan's parents died and Jordan left school. Todd finished high school without Jordan but took every opportunity to go home and see him.

Once university hit Jordan was already way ahead of Todd and was taking his responsibilities very seriously. Todd was the exact opposite and spent his time sleeping, drinking, and having sex. It was in their third year that Todd realized he had to grow up and start preparing for his life. Jordan made Todd realize that he wanted to run his dad's company instead of wasting his life away on booze and women. Not that Todd didn't like booze and women. He definitely did. Jordan made Todd realize his potential and had always held Todd responsible for his actions. He was the only one who did. Todd was lucky to have such a good friend.

Todd, however, did not feel like a very good friend, but Jordan never seemed to think otherwise. Jordan was always forgiving Todd for one stupid thing or another. Jordan never let anything come between him and Todd and never stayed angry, even if Todd deserved it.

Todd had a bad habit of thinking only of himself, which would usually be at the expense of others and Jordan had been on the receiving end of that once or twice. Todd had been working really hard to do better by his friend, and it had been some time since Todd's actions had any effect on his and Jordan's relationship. This changed when Todd met Kate.

Todd didn't think of himself as a stand-up guy, as much as he tried to behave that way. He had a darkness lurking below the surface. Todd had a bit of a twisted mind, OK, to be honest his mind wasn't so much twisted as it was perverted. Sex consumed him. For years, Todd has shared his bed with one night stands, girlfriends who thought they were the only ones, and the random call girl when he didn't feel much like putting in the effort.

Todd lived and breathed sex. He would never admit it to the world but he knew he had an addiction because sex was the first thing he thought about with every girl and the only thing he wanted from them. Todd was known to pick up a woman right off the street, in the grocery store, or in his best friend's office. It had been a while since he attempted to pick up one of Jordan's clients or employees and thought he had kicked that bad habit. Then he met Kate.

Todd fell for Kate the very first time he saw her. He had walked into Jordan's office unannounced, as he always did, to take Jordan out to lunch and there sat this brunette sex pistol. The only thing he could picture was her naked and glistening with sweat calling out his name while he jackhammered her from behind.

"Hey," Todd said, "I was looking for Jordan, sorry, Mr. Best."

"I know him as Jordan, and he just stepped out for a minute," replied the hot piece.

The sound of her voice was perfectly aligned with his fantasy of her and he had to consciously try to control the erection about to explode.

"I see, I'm Todd Oak," he said holding out his hand to shake hers, "Best friend."

"Kate Black," she said, hesitating "I guess our status is dating."

And the bubble of his illusion burst. She's dating Jordan and she should be. Jordan is a catch and I'm a perverted slime ball, Todd thought to himself.

A good friend, and decent guy, would accept that this girl was off the market and move on. Not Todd. He decided that Kate would make a very good fantasy. A fantasy, that quickly turned into an obsession.

Todd's feelings for Kate grew over the years. Of course, he kept them to himself. Todd never wanted to fall in love and start a family but his lust for Kate turned to admiration, admiration to infatuation, infatuation to love. He found he wanted to spend time with her, talk to her about things that were important to her and yes, he wanted to throw her to the ground, tear off her clothes and find himself deep inside of her.

Todd knew how much Jordan loved Kate and could see how Kate loved Jordan in return. So, Todd pined for Kate in silence. However, in his dreams Kate belonged to him. Todd would dream of Kate often, sometimes it felt so real he would wake with the ghost of her still on his skin. The dreams, haunted Todd's waking hours. He could smell her scent lingering as he woke, he could feel her body wrapped around his. He could still hear her screaming out for him to go harder. Todd would wake ready to explode, and so he would shower and finish his dream awake, thinking of Kate.

Todd thought how despicable he is to sit here lusting after Jordan's girl with Jordan lying here in coma, but Todd couldn't help where his mind would go.

Todd would picture Kate kissing Jordan but Todd would turn it into his fantasy and imagine it was him lying in that bed. Todd would imagine he would wake to find Kate over him. Todd would grab her by the back of the neck and yank her to his mouth. He would kiss her until Kate was panting and begging for more. "Todd, I want you, Todd I need you now, Todd…" It was like he could actually hear her saying his name.

"Todd!" Kate said loudly,

"Kate," Todd said startled.

Kate chuckled at him, "Where were you just now?" she asked.

Good lord, he couldn't tell her that. "Not sure just trailed off I guess," Todd said, he stood there taking her in with his eyes, "You look good, rested," he commented.

She did look good. He hadn't seen Kate look more like herself since before the accident.

"You were right to send me there. It was exactly what I needed, kooks and all," Kate told him.

"Kooks?" Todd questioned.

Kate chuckled again, "Nothing, never mind. So obviously, no changes?" she asked.

"No, same old, same old," Todd replied.

Her expression clouded over but quickly returned to this new sunny disposition. This was the Kate he knew and loved.

"So, any "aha" moments while you were away?" asked Todd.

"You could say that," was Kate's reply.

"Care to share?" Todd asked.

"Well, I'm going to stay here for a while and be with Jordan, then I'm going home to unpack and go to sleep. Tomorrow I will get back to a daily life more fitting for me. It may not look like it did before but I'm still figuring things out. I will spend my evenings with Jordan, but I will get back to living my life instead of waiting," Kate responded.

Todd was very happy to hear this and nodded his head in agreement. This would be the first step to Kate moving on, and Todd wanted to be the one that she moved on with. He thought about what that would look like if Jordan did wake up to find Kate with Todd. Would Todd look like a bad friend or would it look like he and Kate found each other during a difficult time in their lives? And would Jordan fight for Kate or leave her to her new life? He didn't hold a candle to Jordan so if Jordan wanted Kate back, it would happen, of that Todd had no doubt.

Todd let this thought linger for a moment before he dismissed it, said his goodbyes, and headed out of the hospital room. Todd's footsteps seemed lighter and he couldn't get the grin off his face because for the first time in two years he had hope, hope he and Kate would find a way into each other's arms.

"Todd!" he heard his name called out. He turned around. It was Kate.

"Sorry I wanted to catch you before you left. I wanted to properly thank you for being here for me. You have taken care of me when I wasn't taking care of myself. You've pushed me to move forward. You've been my rock, you're a good friend and I love you," Kate told Todd and then finished if off with a very tight hug.

Todd bit his tongue so the pain would distract his little brain from reacting to the closeness of her body. His body didn't seem to understand the difference between "dream Kate" and "real Kate" and with all his pent-up excitement it left Todd very reactive. Todd returned the hug quickly, "Of course, anything for you," Todd responded.

Anything at all Todd thought to himself. Food you got it, shoulder to cry on absolutely, a hug on a rough day, it's yours, a lap to cuddle up on, mine is free. Someone to sleep with at night, happy to help. I will hold you, pet you, rub you, lick you and take you like you have never been taken before. Yep, that's dirty, despicable Todd.

Kate pulled away and gave him one last smile before she headed back to Jordan's room. Todd watched her walk away, he watched her behind bounce as she moved down the hall. He watched until she turned and headed into Jordan's room. She gave him one last look and a wave before she was gone.

Then it was Todd's turn to walk away and head for home. With all this daydreaming Todd desperately needed to escape, uninterrupted, into his fantasy. He could feel the weight of all the blood collecting and the dull ache that needed to be released Todd wasn't sure he would make it out of the parking lot. Besides, he thought, it probably wasn't safe to drive with a full load.

So, Todd headed to find a nurse who had some time to kill. It wasn't long before he had one bent over an exam table and was plunging his body into hers. They both climaxed and released. They dressed and Todd promised he would call but he never did.

Chapter 14

Kate returned to Jordan's room. She thought Todd had acted very strange. It made Kate uneasy the way Todd just watched her walk away. She'd never seen that look on his face before. He must have been shocked at her change of personality. Kate had to admit she hadn't exactly been pleasant to be around, always sad and sitting in the dark of Jordan's room. It had to be off-putting for her to leave one way and come back another. Todd must not have thought his plan of sending Kate away would work, and was surprised it had. That could definitely account for his weirdness.

Kate turned her attention back to Jordan. As sad as she was that he was still lying there she had to look at the positive side. He was alive, big positive. He was breathing on his own and he hadn't had a single medical issue since the surgery, aside from not waking. So yes, Kate could restart her life and still have hope that Jordan would wake any day.

"Please baby, wake up soon," Kate said to Jordan.

Kate settled into a chair and began telling Jordan about her weekend. Kate asked rhetorically why Jordan had never told her about the little cabin. She talked about some of the funny pictures she saw of Jordan when he was just a boy. Kate told Jordan how cute she found the little town to be.

"I really want to go back and share that place with you," Kate told Jordan.

Jordan could show her all his favourite spots, and talk about his childhood memories, that was something he did not do too much of. Maybe it was still hard for him to think of a time his parents were alive. Kate could certainly understand that. Her memories of her parents were bittersweet.

Kate had to talk about the crazy psychic lady out loud so, she walked Jordan through the whole story from beginning to end. Laughing again at how absurd the whole thing was.

"I mean, how crazy was she to think I would believe such a tall tale?" Kate asked Jordan.

The day turned into night and Kate decided it was time to go home. Kate wanted to try not sleeping at the hospital anymore. The nurses would call her should there be anything, but after months with no change, Kate doubted they would call. She kissed Jordan goodnight, holding her forehead to his for a moment in silent prayer.

"I'll dream of you," Kate whispered and with one more kiss collected her stuff and headed to her car.

Kate thought the drive home would be hard, that she would feel sick and her heart heavy, as she left Jordan for the first time. She was determined to move forward in life and, at this point, without him. She was sad that he wasn't here but it felt right to move forward, and she felt like Jordan would be okay with that. It wasn't long before she was turning into her driveway and heading into the house.

Entering their house this time seemed different. The house didn't feel so empty and it wasn't quite so quiet. She found she was happy to be there. Kate walked past the suitcases still sitting in the entrance from her weekend away. She'd deal with them later. She wanted to relax and have a long soak in a hot tub.

While upstairs she readied her bath, added lavender oil and bubbles to her water, and decided a glass of wine would make this the perfect way to relax. She went into the kitchen and poured herself a glass of her favourite red wine. Jordan always kept lots of it on hand because it was very hard to get in local stores. Kate took a large gulp of wine feeling the slight burn of the alcohol travel down her throat.

Closing her eyes, she remembered a time when Jordan would have been in the kitchen with her. He'd be telling her about his day, while she got dinner on the table. Jordan made it very difficult to do that task because his arms would always come around her pulling her to him. Kate could still feel that embrace and she smiled, he would do that again. Kate opened her eyes, the kitchen was empty except for the ghost that weighted the air. She sighed and headed back up stairs.

Kate could smell the lavender as she entered her room, and followed the smell until she was settled in the water, bubbles tickling her nose. She had put on upbeat country music and it was playing softly in the background, which made Kate bop to the beat.

Kate soaked a while in the tub, sipping on her glass of wine. She swallowed another gulp and leaned back in the tub, thinking she should probably get out and dry off. Her eyes were getting heavy, and she closed them for a moment to lessen the burn of tiredness. Kate did not realize that instead of just resting them she had fallen asleep.

When Kate opened her eyes, she was confused. She was surrounded by white, there were no walls, or floor, or ceiling it was like she was a character sitting on a blank page waiting for the artist to add more colour. Suddenly, Kate stood before a mirror and saw her reflection. Only her reflection didn't entirely look like her. Then Kate's reflection started talking but there was no sound. The reflection's mouth moved so fast that Kate could not make out a single word. The reflection began waving her hands around wildly and kept pointing up. Kate looked where the reflection was pointing but she didn't see anything.

After a moment, out of nowhere the white started to turn dark, and the dark started falling in slow motion. The reflection of Kate was frantic and seemed terrified of the darkness. The reflection turned sadly and looked away from Kate. Then Kate saw something in the mirror behind the reflection. At first, she couldn't make it out and then it became very clear.

"Jordan!" Kate yelled.

Jordan was trapped in what looked like a glass cube, only he wasn't alone in the cube. There was another man, a man that looked an awful lot like Jordan. Jordan kept banging and running into the translucent wall causing the wall to move but it was like the wall pushed back causing Jordan pain every time. The other man just stood there with his head bowed, it looked like he was defeated, Kate's reflection did as well.

Kate gasped in horror at the injuries being inflicted on Jordan. Tears began to fall down her face. She cried out for Jordan to stop fighting but he couldn't hear her any more than she could hear him. Jordan kept looking to the darkness in fear. It was getting very close now. She could see tears streaming down Jordan's face.

The darkness surrounded Kate and it made her feel like she couldn't breathe. She started choking and coughing but couldn't get any air into her lungs. Kate watched as her reflection fought to get through the mirror. She could see the determination on her reflection's face. The reflection finally did break through the mirrored glass and ran to Kate. She tried to shake the darkness of Kate, but that did nothing. She tried to kick at the darkness but that only made it shake. It almost felt like someone shaking with laughter. Kate could feel the darkness climbing her neck and about to cover her face. Kate's reflection hauled off and smacked the darkness so hard away from Kate's face that she ended up slapping Kate across the face hard.

The sting of the slap jolted Kate from the darkness and at the same time she jolted out of the bath tub of water gasping for air. She climbed out of the tub, throwing herself onto the cold floor gasping and coughing, trying to catch her breath.

After a few moments, Kate collected herself, grabbed a towel from the rack and wrapped herself in it. Now sitting on the floor, her legs shaking, she knew there was no way she was going to be able to stand so she waited and breathed trying to calm her nerves. After a few moments, the shaking lessened, using the wall, she pulled herself up to standing. She stumbled out of the bathroom and threw herself on the bed pulling the blankets around her cold and shaking body.

That was absolutely terrifying, Kate thought. The dream, it just lingered in her thoughts. Jordan was injured, her reflection coming to life, and who was that other man. She had no idea what her subconscious was trying to tell her but whatever it was Kate wasn't sure she wanted to know. Kate finally managed to get warm and her nerves under control. She convinced herself it was just a dream and it meant nothing.

She pulled on a pair of warm pajamas and went into the bathroom to clean up the mess. The floor was covered with water. The glass of wine had broken and the red of the wine bled into the water on the floor. Kate tossed her towel onto the floor to sop up the water. She went over to the tub and pulled the plug, the memory of her almost drowning made her hand shake. Kate did her best to clean up the floor but had no energy left so she threw the towel over the broken wine glass. She would have Lily clean the mess in the morning.

Kate climbed into bed pulling the covers up to her chin because she still had a chill. It felt like a lifetime since she had slept in her own bed. Kate had tried to sleep here a couple of times but found it hard to lay in a bed that she shared with Jordan. It made her miss him so badly. She found the couch to be a better option and had set up camp, avoiding this room as much as possible.

Kate ran a hand over Jordan's side of the bed, his ghost still lingering there. Her eyes started to water and a few tears got loose. She thought about how she'd almost drowned in the tub and the nightmare that came with that. What in the world did it mean? Kate understood why Jordan was being locked away from her. That was obvious. But, why was she seeing a reflection of herself? And who was that man? And what was the darkness? Kate couldn't explain why, but she thought the darkness was a presence trying to consume her.

Was Kate's subconscious trying to tell her something? More likely, it was probably her mind dealing with Jordan's accident and current condition. Her need for Jordan to come back to her all mixed up with the crazy story that the medium told her about another spirit. The spirit being a separate version of Kate that was haunting her.

She really hoped that was the only time she would have that dream. It was hard enough trying to move forward without Jordan but to dream of him like that would make getting back to her life impossible. Kate reluctantly drifted off to sleep hoping her dreams would be of Jordan coming home and not of him caged and suffering.

Chapter 15

Kate had a long night of tossing and turning. She longed for the cabin, and the restful nights she got there. She climbed out of bed groaning, her body stiff and her throat still raw from coughing so hard to get the water out of her lungs. Kate dressed in jogging pants and a t-shirt and dragged herself down to the kitchen to make herself some coffee, hoping that would pick her up.

Kate sat and drank her coffee trying to decide what she was going to do with herself today. She hadn't volunteered in months so she couldn't just show up thinking they needed her. She would have to call them to set up a schedule again. She could start there, but Kate didn't really want to talk to anyone today.

She poured herself another cup of coffee and debated. Maybe she could go shopping, there were a few things she needed. She could go for a walk and just enjoy the sunshine.

Was it even sunny, Kate asked herself. She walked over to the kitchen window and opened the curtains to the bright skies.

It was funny, Kate always loved doing stuff by herself, but her loneliness made her crave companionship now. Right on queue, Kate heard someone rustling around the front door. She wondered who that could be and then she heard the keys. Only one other person had keys to her house and that was Lily.

Lily rounded the corner so preoccupied with her bags that she didn't see Kate sitting at the counter. Once Lily looked up, she jumped and let out a squeal.

"Man, you scared the day lights out of me!" Lily exhaled. "I didn't expect to see you home."

Lily lowered her arm from her chest and breathed.

Kate smiled, "Sorry, I didn't mean to startle you. I came home last night and decided to stay home today. I think I might be around the house a little bit more in the future," Kate said, not sure if she was telling Lily or herself.

"It has been a long time since I have picked up a new book, do you have any recommendations?" Kate asked.

"I have many. Is everything okay? This is a bit of a one-eighty," Lily asked Kate.

"I know, but it's about time. It'll be one day at a time but I'm not doing anyone any good by sitting around all day doing nothing," Kate replied.

"Well, I am glad you're going to be around. I am here if you need anything?" Lily told Kate. "And I do have a very good

novel that I just finished. I'll bring it in next time I'm here."
"Thanks Lily, you're a good friend," Kate replied.

Lily shrugged and headed off to work.

"Lily, I had a bit of an accident last night and I broke a glass in my bathroom. I was so tired that I didn't get around to cleaning it up. Would you mind?" Kate asked.

"Not at all, that's what you pay me the big bucks," Lily replied with a smile.

Lily was an interesting woman. She made a living by cleaning houses and had been with Jordan since he bought this house on his eighteenth birthday. Lily had come highly recommended by one of his friends. She was kind and soft spoken and always had something nice to say.

Lily never really talked about herself and it took a long time for her to open-up to Kate. Lily finally shared that she enjoyed painting and had a few pieces at a local art gallery. Kate called every gallery until she found the right one and went to see Lily's pieces. They were the exact opposite of everything Lily portrayed. They were dark, and intimidating. Very well done but not something Kate would hang in her Livingroom.

"Speaking of big bucks, I've kind of been out of the loop. Have you been getting paid?" Kate asked.

"Yes, Kate, no worries. Andrew had Kurtis oversee the finances to make sure things are taken care of," Lily replied.

"Oh, good," Kate said, she would have to remember to thank Andrew for that foresight. Kate really didn't even think of finances and bills. She's never had to. It looked like there was something else she was going to have to do.

"I think I may go out for a long walk, so, I will be out of your way," Kate told Lily.

"It's a beautiful day for that, enjoy yourself," Lily said and then left the room to get to work.

Watching Lily walk away, she made a mental note to set up a coffee date with Lily real soon.

Kate collected her dishes, put them in the sink and was just about to head out the door when the phone rang. It was so rare that someone would call the house phone that sometimes she forgot they even had one. Kate picked it up cutting off the shrill ring half way through.

"Hello," Kate said into the receiver.

"Well, good morning, you're a hard one to get a hold of. I was wondering what you were up to?" It was Todd on the other end of the line.

Kate wondered why he wasn't calling her on her cell?

"Your cell keeps going to voice mail," Todd said, as if he anticipated her question, "so, I thought I would try the old fashion way and ring you on the tele," he said in, a what was a very poor attempt at, a British accent.

Kate chuckled, she wondered why her cell was going to voicemail and realized she hadn't plugged it to be charged since she had gotten back from her trip.

"I must have forgotten to plug it in," Kate told Todd.

He grunted in acknowledgement, "So what's the plan today?" Todd asked.

"Are you checking up on me," Kate asked teasingly.

"Well, yes, and I wanted to ask if you wanted to go out for a ride?" Todd asked.

"A ride, as in on your bike?" Kate asked getting a little excited.

Todd had a very nice motorcycle and Kate use to jump at the chance to go out for a ride. Her dad would take her out on his bike and they would ride for hours. This memory brought a smile to her face. Kate loved the feeling of life speeding by and the wind blowing all your cares away. It was so freeing. It also helped that it made Jordan absolutely crazy when Todd would pull up on his bike knowing, he would be leaving with her on the back of it.

Jordan was always so worried about them getting into an accident and he was relieved when Kate got home. He would pull her into his arms the minute she was off the bike and she'd remain there the rest of the night which was Kate's favourite part.

Jordan never had anything to worry about. Todd was a very careful driver, always following the rules of the road. He always made sure there was enough distance between them and other vehicles. One thing Kate could say for sure, she always felt safe driving with Todd at the helm.

"That's the idea," Todd announced.

Kate smiled, "That sounds awesome! But don't you have to work?" she asked.

"It was such a nice day I just could not bear the thought of being stuck inside my office. So, I had Judy clear my schedule for the day. I am determined to spend the day driving the countryside, and I just thought I'd see if you wanted to come," Todd explained.

Kate wasn't sure about spending an entire day with Todd. They had never done that before. Usually they would go out for an hour or so on the bike, but this did sound like a perfect thing to do with her day.

"Okay sure, when?" Kate asked Todd.

"I'll see you in thirty," he responded.

They hung up the phone and Kate went back upstairs to put on a pair of jeans and her leather jacket. The leather jacket was a gag gift Todd had given her for Christmas. He had it personalized and it read "His biker chick".

Todd had tried and tried to get Jordan to buy a bike and come out for a ride with him many times, but Jordan absolutely refused to own a bike. So, the only person Kate could and would ride with was Todd. The jacket was another play to convince Jordan he needed to get a bike, but Jordan didn't bite. They all had a good laugh about the jacket and now it was a ritual, Kate had to wear it every time she and Todd went for a ride.

Kate liked remembering the good times she shared with Jordan. She wished Jordan would be at home anxiously awaiting her return. Knowing that wasn't the case, she sighed and headed for the front door to wait for Todd to come roaring up the street.

It was a nice day out, the sun was shining, not a cloud in the sky. It was quite hot, and Kate thought if Todd didn't get here soon the jacket was coming off. Just as she was about to give into the heat she heard the thunder of Todd's motorcycle coming down the street.

Todd's motorcycle was black and chrome, shinning brightly in the sun. He was wearing blue jeans and a black leather jacket too. Todd wasn't a small man and seeing him pulling up onto her drive, for the first time, she realized how intimidating he could look. Then he pulled off his helmet and all that intimidation fell away because of the silly child like grin on his face.

Kate chuckled, this big burly man was nothing but a big old teddy bear. Kate gave Todd a wave and was about to walk to join him on the drive when Lily exited the house. Lily stopped short when she saw Todd and his motorcycle.

"Are you going for a ride with him?" Lily asked, her look questioning.

"Yeah, it's been a while but Todd and I would do this every occasionally," Kate responded.

"I see," Lily replied.

Kate didn't understand Lily's reaction. She must be concerned about the bike.

"Don't worry Lily, Todd is an excellent driver," Kate said to try to reassure her.

"Good, okay, have fun," Lily responded seeming to snap out of whatever mood she was in.

Lily headed down the drive to her car parked on the street. Todd eyed her as she left.

"Please don't tell me you need to run your plans by your maid," Todd asked sarcastically.

Kate punched Todd in the arm.

"Lily is my friend and she was just concerned, not everyone likes motorcycles," Kate responded.

"You're right, just the cool kids," he returned, punching Kate right back.

Kate rubbed her arm, his punch was definitely harder then hers.

"Are we going to stand around admiring your bike or are we going to ride it?" Kate asked.

"Jump on biker chick, let's make some dust," Todd shouted happily.

"Okay, okay!" Kate replied.

Kate climbed on and the bike came to life. They headed out onto the street to some unknown destination, Kate took a deep breath. Her body and mind calm and ready to be free on the open road.

Chapter 16

Todd took his bike out on the road. The thunder was loud in his ears. He loved riding his bike and took it out every chance he got. Todd spent so much time cooped up in his office, often spending longs grueling hours working on one project or another. It was freeing to get out on the open road and just drive. Todd never had a destination in mind, he would just end up lost somewhere and then continued to drive until he found home. His bike was like a horse, it always eventually pointing its way home.

Todd turned down Kate's street, he looked to see if she was outside. There she was on the drive so he pulled in and shut down his bike. Todd watched Kate as she walked over to join him. Kate looked so freaking sexy, when she would join him for a ride. Kate wore skinny jeans, that tucked themselves neatly into a pair of black boots. She wore the leather jacket he had gotten her for Christmas. Everyone thought it was a joke and a way to get a rise out of Jordan, but secretly it was

Todd's way of turning his fantasy about Kate to reality, even if it was only his reality.

Just as Kate was about to reach him, Kate's maid, came outside. She gave Todd a dirty look and then looked at Kate with judgment. Kate and the maid spoke. He could hear Kate reassuring her that Todd was a good driver. What the heck? Did Kate have to justify going out with him to the maid? Todd thought angrily. Kate needs to put that woman in her place but Kate was too nice.

"Hey! Let's go!" Todd called out.

Kate looked so good, Todd could not wait to get her straddled in behind him.

Kate gave the maid a wave goodbye.

"Okay, Okay," Kate relied and climbed up on the bike.

Todd and Kate teased each other. Todd was too distracted by Kate's appearance to process what was being said.

Todd took off with a jolt, forcing Kate to wrap her arms around his waist tight. Eventually she loosened her grip and held onto the bars in the back. Occasionally Todd accelerated fast causing Kate's arms to return around him. Todd would chuckle, and so would Kate. Kate probably thought he was just playing with her and he was, but his impetus was far more deviant than she thought.

They drove down country road after country road, checking out the scenery. There were ponds, and fields of corn. Kate would always point out the farms with animals. They finally turned into a small town outside of the city. They decided to grab some lunch and found a small diner. The pair entered the diner and ordered burgers and fries off a very limited menu. The place was a dive and lacked charm but, to Todd's surprise, the food was delicious.

Kate and Todd talk about stuff they had done in the past and their plans for the future. Kate was joking, laughing and poking fun at Todd. She was in a really good mood. It felt good to be carefree, it felt good to be with Kate like this.

Once they finished eating they took the bike back out on the road. They drove around the town and then back out onto the country roads. Todd was really enjoying his day with Kate and could see them doing this all the time. He didn't want it to end but then he felt her tap him on the shoulder. He pulled over and lifted his shield.

"It's time for me to head over to the hospital," Kate told him.

Todd nodded and dropped his shield. He was disappointed. He didn't want her to go. Todd brooded for a few minutes and decided to tap the accelerator to the bar, jolting the bike forward, and like always her arms came around his waist. He could feel her body shaking with laughter and loved that he was the cause of it.

It wasn't long before Todd pulled up in front of the hospital and Kate dismounted from the bike. She handed him the helmet. Her face was red from the heat and her hair a wild mess. Todd had pictured her that way so many times, but not under these circumstances.

"Thanks for the day. I was procrastinating, and trying to find something to do. I wasn't ready to dive into figuring out what's next in my life," Kate confided in him.

"Glad I could help, call on me anytime," Todd responded. "To be honest, I'm very lonely, my best friend is in a coma."

"Really? What a coincidence so is mine," Kate retorted. "Misery loves company, we could keep each other company," she suggested jokingly.

Kate may have only been joking but Todd was glad she said it because that was defiantly the plan.

Kate gave him a wave good bye and headed into the hospital. Todd pretended to fiddle with his bike but really, he just wanted to watch Kate walk away. Once Kate entered the front doors and was out of sight, Todd put the bike in drive and roared down the hospital laneway. The plan was to head home but he was so energized by the day he had, he wasn't ready to go home.

Todd sat at the stop sign trying to decide what to do and which way to go. He finally decided to visit his brother. Between work and Jordan Todd had not spent much time with Vick.

Todd forced his bike to life and headed to his brother's apartment. The apartment was in a run-down part of town. Todd never understood why Vick lived there. Their parents had large trust funds set up for them, which was their way of saying "I love you" since the traditional one took emotion. Todd wasn't even sure if his parents even loved each other because they didn't show it.

Vick tried very hard not to touch his trust fund. He went to nursing school and got a job at the hospital. It drove their parents crazy to see their son of means, working a low status job, and to add salt to a wound their parents absolutely despised having to visit Vick in that side of town.

The security door was propped open, allowing Todd access to the building without having to announce himself over the intercom. Todd rolled his eyes and thought. "So much for security!" He headed to the stairs and took the steps two at a time. His pace slowing as he neared the top of the third floor. Todd pushed through the fire door and walked down the hall until he stood in front of Vick's door.

Todd knocked on the door, but no one answered. There was loud music coming from inside. Vick probably didn't hear him, Todd thought. Todd walked over to the window that overlooked the parking lot to see if Vick's car was there. Todd had gotten into trouble the last time he walked into Vick's apartment unannounced.

Vick's car was there so Todd tried the door knob, it was unlocked. Of course it's unlocked Todd thought to himself, rolling his eyes. Vick was just the perfect target for a crazed person. Todd stepped into the apartment and was greeted by the boom boom of loud music.

"Vick?" Todd called out but there was no response so he headed into the living room and called out again. Todd heard a bang and Vick curse. Vick poked his head out the bedroom door.

"Todd? What the heck are you doing here?" Vick asked irritated.

Todd raised an eyebrow, "I wanted to see if my little brother wanted to have dinner tonight? I knocked but the music must have drowned out the sound."

"The music isn't why I did not hear you knock," Vick responded sarcastically. "Just a minute," he said and then closed the door.

A few minutes later Vick came into the living room, Todd had turned down the music and seated himself on the sofa. Todd looked up and realized why Vick hadn't heard him knock. He was accompanied by a brunette woman, looking quite dishevelled. She was hot. Too bad she was one of his brother's conquests or Todd would have definitely hit on her.

The brunette gave Vick a kiss and a wink. Vick smacked her on the butt as she headed for the door. It was weird but the brunette reminded him of Kate. They shared similar features, or Todd just had Kate on the brain?

"Impeccable timing as always big brother," Vick said, sarcasm dripping off his words.

Todd shrugged, "my bad" he said. Then he grabbed his little brother in a bear hug and squeezed. "Well you must be starved after your workout so where do you want to eat?"

Laughing, Vick surrendered his bad mood, "I like a big burger after a good ravishing. How about Frankie's?" Vick suggested.

"Perfect," replied Todd, "You want to jump on the back of my bike?" Todd asked.

Vick gave him a repulsed look, "No! I will never get onto that death trap. I see way too many tragedies at the hands of a motorcycle and I hate that you and Kate have some misguided obsession with them," he said.

Todd gave a shrug, "Meet you there then?"

"I'll be there in ten," Vick replied.

The two brothers met at the diner they referred to as their "dinning room" because they ate there so often. They ordered their usual meals and dug in. They chatted about Vick's love life and Todd's lack of one. Todd never admitted to anyone that he did, in fact, have a playmate, that he quite enjoyed.

Todd told Vick that he and Kate spent most of the day out on his bike. Vick was surprised that Kate peeled herself away from Jordan. Todd explained that Kate returned from her trip renewed and ready to move on. Todd left out the part about Kate spending every evening with Jordan. He didn't tell Vick because Todd wanted to put his head in the sand and hold onto the thought that he and Kate would be together. Thinking of Jordan made Todd feel guilty and ashamed, so he tried to spend very little time thinking about how bad a friend he was.

Todd sat back and remembered how Kate looked after pulling off her helmet. Her face was flushed from the warmth of the helmet and her hair disheveled. That made Todd's mind wander to his fantasy where he had Kate lying on her back in his bed, her body heated from the passion between them. Todd wanted to see Kate again.

At that moment, it occurred to Todd that Kate did not have her car and would have to take a taxi home, unless a gentleman were kind enough to go and pick her up. Okay, so Todd was no gentleman but nobody needed to know that and it would give Todd an excuse to see Kate again.

Todd thanked Vick for joining him for dinner. He stood and gave Vick a punch on the arm, waved and headed out of the diner. Todd jumped on his bike and thundered down the road towards the hospital. He wasn't sure if Kate would still be there, but he hoped she was. He parked his bike and headed in to find out.

Chapter 17

Vick sat back in the booth thinking about Kate moving on with her life. Todd had told him that Kate came back from her weekend renewed. Vick had a love, hate relationship with Kate. Vick loved Kate and hated himself for it.

Kate was far from the woman he thought he wanted in life but, he was so drawn to her. He had very little control when he was around her and all he wanted to do was touch her. So, for Jordan's sake, he forced himself to stay away from Kate. Which was a difficult task.

When Vick was forced to be around her, he would be in so much pain that all he could do was be abrupt, critical and overbearing. It was so hard lately, that it took all he had to remain at a distance. Kate is Jordan's girl. Well, was Jordan's girl, now who knows.

Vick didn't understand why he felt so strongly about Kate, but he had since the first time they met. Kate didn't remember the first time they met, but he sure did. In fact, they had crossed paths before Todd and Jordan ever did.

Vick and Kate did not meet under the best of circumstances. It was the afternoon Kate had lost her parents and she had run into the ER, just as she did after Jordan's accident. Rushing to the nurse's station, Vick could still see the hope in Kate's eyes. The hope that her parents were ok. Vick's eyes could not leave Kate and it pained Vick to know what Kate was about to find out.

Vick was glad he wasn't the one having to deliver the bad news, because he's not sure he could and remain professional. He remembers the shrill of Kates scream, how it sent chills through his body. Vick watched as Kate's legs gave out and her body fell to the floor, the doctor catching her just as she was about to hit the floor.

Vick's heart went out to Kate like it would to anyone who lost someone they loved in such a tragic and violent way, but his feelings were more then that. Vick had never felt like that before and feeling that way for a stranger was even more bizarre.

Vick was asked to help Kate into a chair and to watch for symptoms of shock. Kate sat without moving, or speaking, he was watching her chest rise and fall to make sure she was still breathing. After a while, Vick was relieved by another nurse. He left, exhausted, to get a cup of coffee and breathe himself.

After awhile he headed back to work and found that Kate was talking to the nurse sitting with her.

"Where are they?" Kate asked the nurse caring for her.

"They have been brought to the morgue. When you're ready, I can take you there," the nurse spoke softly.

Kate shook her head and stood with the aid of the nurse. Vick found himself wanting to take the nurses place with Kate.

"I'm ok, let's go," Kate said quietly.

"Are you sure?" the nurse asked. "Is there anyone I can call for you?"

"No," Kate replied, short.

The nurse nodded and they headed down the hall. Vick wanted to follow but at that moment another trauma was brought in from an ambulance. Vick snapped out of his trance and his training kicked in, he was back to work. Kate didn't cross his mind again until the nurse, Cindy, told him that Kate had sat down outside of the morgue doors and was refusing to budge until her parents' bodies were transported to the funeral home.

Vick had a feeling that if given the choice, Kate would have sat in the morgue with her parents. The only time Kate would move or look up was when someone entered or exited the damp, cold room.

Kate's parents had to have autopsies and it took three days for them to be released to the funeral home. During that time, Vick made any excuse he could so he would have to walk by the morgue. He picked up as many shifts as he could get, often working doubles just to be close to Kate, who barely moved from that chair.

He was dumbfounded by this brunette. Normally he was attracted to blondes and found the odd redhead fiery. Kate did not have the curvy body that Vick usually went for and she was more uptown then he liked. Vick liked a good set of boobs, a firm plump butt and a girl who would slum it. He had no idea, what it was about this woman that caught his attention. It was like Vick had no freewill and was pulled into Kate's atmosphere by some cosmic force.

Vick finally got the nerve to talk to Kate again, just before her parents were transported out of the hospital. She was sitting unmoving in front of the double doors, her head bowed low not looking up at anyone that passed by. Vick was on his way to the lab to drop off samples, which was not his job. Vick grabbed the samples and said he would take them and walked away with the head nurse staring after him like he was insane.

Vick knew he shouldn't stop, he had a feeling he should leave her alone. That she was going to be trouble, but maybe that was what the attraction was. Vick lost all control of his body and found himself seated beside Kate. He just needed to help Kate, he couldn't bear seeing her in so much pain.

"I'm very sorry for what you're going through?" Vick said.

"Your loss," replied Kate without looking up.

"Pardon?" asked Vick, unsure what she meant.

"You're suppose to say, I'm sorry for your loss," replied Kate emotionless.

"Well, who am I to know for sure? A friend of mine lost his parents, he told me how much he hated when people said that to him, it drove him crazy. So, I have made it a point not to say that anymore to people who have suffered a loss," Vick offered.

Kate was silent for a long time before she spoke.

"Thanks," was all Kate said, then stood to look through the double doors again.

Vick remained seated waiting for Kate to return to her seat. Kate hesitated but did sit back down.

"Can I get you anything? Something to eat or drink?" Vick asked.

"No, thank you," Kate replied.

Vick sat with her in silence for a few more minutes. As Vick was about to leave, Kate spoke.

"I'm sorry if I am being rude, but I'm having a very hard time finding words or coming up with a coherent sentence," Kate said.

Vick wanted nothing more then to pull Kate into his arms and hold her until she found strength, but he was a total stranger to her. Just as Vick was about to respond to Kate. Two attendants dressed in suits started to pull gurneys from the morgue that held Kate's parents. They were loaded into the back of two black SUV's with tinted windows.

"I guess they don't use hearses anymore," Kate commented.

"No, not for this part. It makes things a little more private for the families in mourning," Vick offered.

One of the attendants came through the double doors and handed Vick a clipboard.

Kate stood there looking at the two black SUV's. It was minutes before they were drove out of sight.

"What will you do now?" Vick asked.

Kate looked at Vick like he was asking her the hardest question in the world.

"What do I do?" Kate repeated. "I'm told life goes on," she said.

Kate turned and walked away looking like she was carrying the weight of the world. Vick never dreamed he would see Kate again, but life is funny that way and here she was tormenting his very existence.

Vick still longed to have Kate in his arms, to look at him the way she looked at Jordan. No one knew that but him, and Kate didn't remember him at all. Vick didn't want her to remember him and see him as the nurse who watched her parents get carted off. It was a tragic time for Kate and not the best footing to start a relationship on, even if that relationship was just a friendship. Only they weren't friends at all. Kate tolerated Vick and Vick was a jerk to Kate.

Vick wanted to treat her better and be there for her like Todd was, but he couldn't control his actions when he was around her. His behaviour just made Kate dislike him even more. Isn't it a saying that when a boy pulls girl's pigtails on the playground it means that they like them? Vick thought. Well, yank, yank.

It probably was for the best that Vick and Kate were not close. Vick wanted Kate badly, but he cared for his friend, and he knew that if Jordan were to wake Kate would never leave him. If he doesn't wake, then they would all lose someone they loved and moving on from that tragedy would be next to impossible.

Vick sighed as he walked the rest of the way to his car. It was a nice night so he decided to go for a drive. The air had a nice chill, which was refreshing. He let it roll over his face, it cooled his hot skin. Vick wished there was some way he could get this girl out of his head and find someone who could return his affections. That seemed impossible. No one seemed to compare. Vick resigned to his fate of everlasting longing and heartache and headed for home.

Once at his apartment, he needed a cool drink and sat down with a glass of whiskey, leaving the bottle in front of him. He didn't work the next day so he could afford a night he would forget. Before things got too out of control and Vick drunk dialed Kate, he thought it would be best to call in a distraction. Vick was currently dating a couple of very nice ladies so he picked up his phone, opened his contacts, and with a flick of his finger scrolled through the list of names. He would call the first one that came up.

Vick selected call and waited for the phone to ring.

"Hello?" came a female voice.

"Michelle!" Vick said happily into the phone.

"Vick?" Michelle replied.

"Yes, I am feeling lonely, baby. Can you come over?" Vick asked in a sad voice.

"So, you call me out of the blue and want me to come over at the drop of a hat. What if I had plans?" Michelle asked in a tone.

"Then I would continue to be lonely," replied Vick.

Vick heard Michelle sigh and he knew she was defeated. "I think your bad news, Vicks" She said and paused, "but I'll be over soon."

Vick smiled, "You're the best baby".

Vick sat back and finished his drink. It was more fun to drink with someone else. He had planned on killing that bottle, and then drowning himself in carnal pleasure, with Michelle who would make a very sexy partner in crime. He waited impatiently to hear the rap of Michelle's hand on his door.

Chapter 18

Kate sat in Jordan's room listening to the beep of his heart rate monitor. She just finished a sandwich from the cafeteria. Kate had a good day with Todd, and shared it with Jordan. She found herself thinking about Todd. He had been very kind and great company. There were times today when she found herself wanting him to touch her arm or hold her hand. This was really causing Kate to have conflicted feelings. She must really be starved for attention, Kate thought, and Todd was a close friend. That was all it was, Kate reassured herself.

She leaned back in the uncomfortable hospital chair, it was getting close to nine and she should head home soon. Kate should have gone home first but she was so elated and conflicted from the ride with Todd she wasn't thinking about how she would get home at the end of the day.

The beep of the monitor became a sound far off in the distance and she felt all her thoughts slowly fading away. Kate began to dream of she and Todd laughing and sitting on her couch. Todd ran a hand down her face and told Kate how beautiful she was. Kate leaned into his hand, her body pulling her forward until she was wrapped into Todd's arms. He squeezed her tightly. She could feel his breath in her hair. She wanted to pull him on top of her, she wanted his lips hard on hers. Todd sat back and looked Kate in the eyes. She could see how badly he wanted her. All of a sudden, she felt a hand on her shoulder, she turned to look and there was Jordan saying her name. Kate looked back to Todd sitting on the couch and was confused.

"Kate," Jordan said again, the hand shaking her shoulder.

"Kate!" She sat up with a start and tried to focus her vision. The room came into view and Kate found Todd kneeling beside her chair his face not far from hers. It took Kate a moment to realize she had been dreaming, but the feeling of want sat between them.

Todd smiled at her, "Sorry, didn't mean to frighten you. I just stopped by to see if you wanted a ride home?" he asked.

Kate's body relaxed, grateful that Todd did not seem to notice her awkwardness.

"Thank you, but you didn't have to interrupt your night to come back here. I could have taken a cab," Kate replied.

"Please, it was no interruption," Todd told Kate, "I was just coming from dinner with Vick and like a gentleman thought I'd offer you a ride home," Todd said with a twinkle in his eye.

"Oh, so no hot date tonight?" Kate asked teasingly.

Todd chuckled, ignoring her question, "Are you ready to go?"

Kate nodded and collected her things, stuffed them into her coat pocket and kissed Jordan goodnight. She followed Todd out to his bike. They put on their helmets, mounted the bike, and were off into the night.

The air was chilly which was a big difference from the warm hospital room and Kate was shivering. Without thinking she put her arms around Todd and leaned into him for the warmth of his body. He placed his hand over hers holding them for a moment then gave them a tap and returned to the task of driving.

Kate, found she liked her arms around Todd. It gave her stomach butterflies when he put his hand on hers. She was disappointed when he returned them to the bars.

They pulled into her drive and Todd turn off the ignition. She handed him her helmet and thanked him again. The ride had woken her up for a few reasons and she wasn't quite sure what to do until she was ready for bed.

"So, what's your plan now? Heading home? You must have an early day at the office since you played hooky today?" Kate asked dragging out their goodbye. She just didn't feel like going inside to be alone just yet.

"Not sure, I may sit down with a movie and popcorn. Work, well its work, that's why I have minions," Todd winked at her.

Kate smiled in return, a movie and popcorn did sound good. "I may steal that idea, haven't seen a new flick in...'" she trailed off thinking of the movie she and Jordan saw right before his accident. "Well, you know," Kate said and shrugged at Todd.

Todd nodded and dismounted his bike. "Well, do you feel like company?" he asked.

Kate smiled at Todd. She wanted that, but at the same time she was terrified about what that meant. This was Jordan's best friend. He was being kind and she was being, what? Lonely, she told herself. She was building this up in her own head and she just needed a reality check. They were friends and a movie would be great.

"That would be nice," Kate replied and headed to the front door. Todd followed leaning up against the side of the house watching Kate as she unlocked the deadbolt.

Once inside they headed to the kitchen to make popcorn and Kate looked in the fridge for some beer. There were a few left from before Jordan's accident. Kate wasn't much of a beer drinker but she liked to have one every once in awhile. Kate handed one to Todd, who popped the cap of his bottle and then reached over placing his hand on hers and popped the cap off. Kate smiled to thank him. She thought if she spoke in that moment her voice was sure to crack giving away everything going on onside her head.

While they previewed the movie selection on Kate's TV guide they spoke about the weather and their plans for the next week. Kate asked Todd if Vick would join him for what Todd called his "quarterly dinner" with his parents.

Todd chuckled, "Well, if he can pull himself away from his extra-curricular activities, he might," Todd grabbed the popcorn and threw some in his mouth.

Kate lifted an eyebrow at the way Todd said, "extra-curricular".

Todd told Kate about walking into Vick's apartment because he didn't think Vick heard him knock on the door. Then explained how he had interrupted the wrestling match, the ring being Vick's bed.

"I'll give him this, he has impeccable taste in women. The chick was hot!" Todd said with a wink.

Kate rolled her eyes at Todd, and they both laughed.

"Vick was none too happy with my interruption, but a bear hug from the big guy," Todd said with double thumbs, "and a promise of dinner at Frankie's, all was forgiven."

Kate laughed, remembering this was not the first-time Todd got into trouble for walking into Vick's apartment without warning.

"You really have to stop walking in like you own the place. One of these times your going to walk into a scenario that will be burned into your skull forever," Kate said.

Todd also laughing, "You're not wrong" he admitted.

They settled on a movie that seemed to have action, comedy and romance and sat back sharing the coffee table as a foot rest and the bowl of popcorn between them. The movie started out great but Kate ended up being more tired then she thought and ended up falling asleep on the couch. She could hear the rumble of the TV as she slipped away.

Kate was jolted awake for the second time tonight by Todd, as he was trying to place a blanket over her. Kate looked up at him leaning over her pausing halfway through his task of covering her. She thought he had a weird look in his eye but dismissed it. She removed the blanket, standing to stretch.

"So how was the movie?" Kate asked Todd.

"It was more a romantic comedy than action," he responded grumpily.

Kate chuckled, "Oh, poor baby," she replied.

"I was just about to head out," Todd told Kate.

"I'll walk you out," Kate motioned towards the door.

Kate opened the front door for Todd, "Thanks for hanging out, it was nice," she said to Todd.

Todd nodded.

"We should do this more often, I mean I know your Jordan's best friend but you've become more to me over these last few months and I feel like I can be myself with you. The good, the bad and the ugly," Kate confided, hoping her words came out friendly and not in a way that gave away the other feelings she had been having.

"I feel the very same Kate. I find that when I want to call Jordan and can't, I dial your number," Todd making a confession of his own.

This made Kate's heart skip a beat, "Well, misery does love company," Kate replied.

"So, tomorrow then," Todd wink at her.

Kate laughed, "Why not?"

Todd gave a wave. Jumping on his bike and took off down the street.

Kate watched him as the blackness of the night swallowed him, making her think of the dream she had of the darkness falling on her. The dream where Jordan was locked in a cage. The reminder of this made Kate's heart ache. She missed him and wanted him here.

Man, this dream just kept crawling back into her mind. She shook her head, with one more look up the street, she closed the door and headed upstairs to bed. Lying in bed she found herself thinking of Todd and Jordan. She loved Jordan, of this she was sure, but what were the feelings she was having about Todd. Todd has been kind, and helpful and a good friend and she missed Jordan for so many reasons. She was feeling lonely in her bed wanting Jordan to be with her. She missed his arms and the feeling of his naked body against hers.

Kate was lonely for companionship and needed to feel the love of a man and because Todd was the only one around she was confusing her affections for him. Jordan was the man she loved and Todd was just a friend.

"He is just a friend," Kate said out loud, then rolled over in an attempt to sleep.

Chapter 19

$\mathcal{T}$odd left Kate's house with an ache that needed to be satisfied. He was getting a strange vibe from her and it made his body come to life. Pulling to the side of the road, he whipped out his cell phone and dialed.

"Hello," came a female voice from the other end on the line.

"Hey, it's Todd, do you have any plans tonight?" he asked.

"Todd? Oh, no, actually you're in luck, my plans for tonight just got cancelled last minute," said the female.

"Great so my place, 20 minutes?" Todd asked.

"Okay, should I bring anything?" she asked.

"Nope, I have it all taken care of," Todd replied.

The female voice chuckled, "Yes, you always do. I'll see you in twenty."

Todd ended the call and steered his bike in the direction of home, a smile spread across his face. His night was about to get even better.

Todd reached his building, parked his bike underground and headed to the elevator. He got off the elevator, to find his guest was already waiting in his entrance. She was leaning against the wall and he could see the very feminine curves of her body. His body yearned to feel those curves against him. He could take her right now in the entrance if she had been dressed in what he liked, but that was kept safe and sound inside his apartment.

Todd looked his guest over, it had taken him so long to find the perfect girl that could fill his fantasies and with a few tweaks she transformed into the very thing he wanted most in this world. The woman sauntered over and was about to give him a kiss hello, when Todd stopped her.

"Ah, ah," he waved a naughty finger in front of her face.

The woman was not phased by this and chuckled.

She ignored him and pushed her body against his, "Your wish is my command," she said.

He bumped her back with his pelvis and walked the rest of the way to his door. Todd opened the door and directed her to the bedroom down the hall.

"You know where to find it?" he asked.

"Yes I do," she said nodding and sauntered off. Todd watched her as she walked, she even walked the right way, he thought to himself. Todd busied himself in the kitchen, opening some wine and pouring it into two glasses almost to the rim. He took the glasses and headed in the opposite direction of the woman to his bedroom.

Todd, entering his room set the glasses down on the dresser and turned on some music. The music played low, and he stripped down, pulling on just his robe and tying it loosely around his waist. He drank down about half his glass before a knock rapped on the bedroom door.

"Todd, Baby," whispered the female. Her voice was the only thing that wasn't quite right, but it worked in a whisper. "Can I come in?" she asked.

Todd walked over swinging the door open wide blocking her entrance, looked down at his companion and smiled. Her hair had changed to the perfect shade of brown, her blue eyes now twinkled at him green. Her lips painted a warm pink, she wore no other make up. She too wore nothing but a robe.

She stepped into him, and ran her hands over his bare chest. Feeling her fingers on his skin brought him to life.

"Well, I wondered what was taking so long?" Todd asked eyeing her.

Without missing a beat, "Just trying to be perfect for you, my love, I only want to please," she said.

That's right baby, he thought, you play your part well. He pulled her into his embrace and began to kiss her greedily. She returned his kiss with as much enthusiasm. Her scent in his nose was sweet with a hint of lavender. Man, how he loved that smell.

Without any notice, she pushed him away, "Now, now, baby, What's the rush? I am here all night," she said coyly.

She walked around him, her hand trailing along his body as she did. Then it travelled south and she began to rub. Todd moaned in pleasure and grabbed her wrist. She pulled away.

"Hands to yourself mister," she whispered to him.

He put his hands up in surrender and she began to rub him again. Todd held his hands up for as long as he could before he could bare it no longer. As his hands came down she stopped. Walking over to the dresser, she seated herself beside the wine glasses. Her legs wide open the robe falling was the only thing that hid her treasure.

Todd walked over and placed himself between her legs pushing his groin into hers. The only thing stopping him from taking her was the satin between them. But Todd pushed his length against her as hard as he could and could feel the material and the tip of him entering the beginning of her body. She threw her head back in pleasure and moaned. Her robe fell down her arms exposing her breast, her nipples already hard. Todd licked his finger and ran a hand over one of her nipples, circling it and then pinching before he did the same to the other. She moaned again. Todd loved the way that sounded.

But then she stopped and pushed Todd away. He stumbled back a few steps before he righted his footing. As he did, she had climbed off the dresser and came to stand in front of him.

"If you keep doing that I am going to turn you over and punish you," Todd said firmly.

She was not phased by his tone or words, "Me? Oh, I would never need to be punished," she said.

She took his hand and led him over the edge of the bed and pushed him onto it. She straddled him and he sat up wrapping his arms around her. She began to grind on him, and then she leaned in and began kissing him, gently at first and then harder, her grinding became fast and hard and it took everything for Todd not to throw her down and slam himself into her.

Todd's pleasure climbed until he was almost at his breaking point, noticing this she slowed and then dismounted to stand. She looked down at him. Todd placed his head between her breast and nuzzled them with his nose. Breathing heavy, he pulled her pelvis against him and began to remove her robe. She stopped him and stepped back. Slowly she untied the belt and let the robe slide down her body teasingly, her eyes not leaving his. She smiled wickedly at Todd. Coyly, she slipped the robe back on and turned to walk away.

"We need some more wine," she said, about to go grab a glass.

Todd grabbed her arm and yanked her to him.

"Oh, no you don't," he said. "I have had just about enough of that."

Before she could even say a word, Todd ripped the robe from her body and took her from behind.

"You better hold on," he warned.

She grabbed the bed post. Todd held her from behind and slammed his body into her, hard and fast.

She cried out in pleasure, her body bouncing off his in return to his thrusts, both their climaxes growing until Todd was on the edge of sweet explosion.

"Yes, yes, oh Todd," she cried out from her own explosion, and he could feel her body pulse around his.

This sent Todd over the edge and he released his tension calling out her name too.

"Oh, Kate!"

Spent they collapsed onto the bed. After catching their breath, they climbed underneath the blankets, her head resting on his chest. They laid there listening to the music. She ran a finger up and down his chest each stroke getting longer and longer until she was bringing his body back to life.

She climbed onto him and began rocking, not letting him enter her. Todd ran his hands over her smooth skin and then rested them on her hips. After a few minutes, he was breathing heavily again and was ready to feel the warmth of her swallow him again. He guided her body over his until he was entering her body. This time the movements were slow and gentle. They enjoyed the pleasure of each other for a very long time. Once they both climaxed, they curled into each other. He buried his face in her hair. He fell asleep thinking about Kate, pretending, it was her in his arms. His dreams full of what would never be.

Chapter 20

Kate woke the next day, determined to return to her normal schedule. She started volunteering at her usual places and everyone was happy to see her back. It was difficult at first trying to fall into a life that now felt like it belonged to someone else, but Kate toughed it out and it all became her normal again.

With a need to keep herself busy, she added reading to patients in the hospital. Sick, elderly, or in a coma like Jordan, it didn't matter. She would go in and read whatever books wanted, which could be awkward when it had racy bits. Volunteering still gave her a sense of worth. Proud that she was giving back to her community.

Kate still struggled with her "off" day. These days, she would hang out with Todd, and sometimes even Vick. She and Vick had never been true friends, and Kate never understood why. She tried to be nice when they first met, but it got to the point where she couldn't stand to be around him. Avoiding each other was hard to do with mutual friends. The funny thing is there would be these moments, where Vick was kind and warm. Then his mood swing would happen making Kate's head spin.

Kate enjoyed hitting the road with Todd on his bike. They would drive around hitting little shops and diners along the way. Sometimes they stayed at home, hers or Todd's, having drinks and listening to music. They could just sit in comfortable silence. Kate stopped thinking about her feelings for Todd and just enjoyed his company. She hadn't had that type of comfort with anyone except Jordan.

Todd and Kate found they had a lot more in common then they realized. Going out on the bike for one, eating mayo with their fries and gravy, was another. Todd loved a good stand-up comedy show and so did Kate. They also both shared Kate's love of board games and each with a competitive nature.

On the odd occasion, Kate, Todd and Vick would get together. They would all go to dinner at Frankie's and usually close the place down. Tommy, the actual owner of Frankie's, would personally serve their table. They had become so regular over the years that Tommy would often join their table. He appeared to have a strange obsession with Todd. Always asking many personal questions.

Kate still spent every evening with Jordan, talking to him like he was actually listening. She would recall events from her day, laughing as she told him stories. Kate was beginning to settle into her new way of life.

It had been months since the accident and seasons had changed twice, it was the end of fall and winter look liked it would be here early.

"It really looks like it's going to snow," she commented to Jordan.

Kate was standing at the window looking out over all the people hurrying by, their coats pulled up to their noses.

"I remember you telling me that you liked the first snow fall. It made you feel like a kid again," Kate continued to talk.

"I bet you and Todd had snowball fights all the time, and I bet Vick would always win," Kate laughed. "That guy can appear out of thin air," she said.

Just like that, Vick came waltzing in the room.

"Hey," he said.

"Hi. Your ears must have been burning," Kate said to Vick.

"No, why would they be?" Vick asked defensively.

"Oh nothing," Kate sighed, "just reminiscing. "What brings you in?"

"Got called in, nurse on this floor is off with the flu that is going around, as bunch of others have it too. So, here I am!"

He marched through the room. Vick looked over Jordan's machine, he stood looking at Jordan for a moment, then turned his attention to Kate.

"My name is Vick and I'll be your nurse this evening, if you need anything please don't hesitate to ask," Vick said mockingly and left the room.

Vick had never been assigned to Jordan before. He usually worked the emergency room. It was a rare occasion you would find Vick in any other wing. I guess a large portion of the nursing staff being sick with the flu would count as a rare occasion.

Kate sat down in the chair beside Jordan's bed to read him a novel she knew he would hate. She had just cracked the spine when she heard the commotion in the hall.

"No, I am not okay with this!" screamed a female voice. "He should still be upstairs with the specialist," she continued her voice getting more hysterical.

Kate stood and walked towards the door until she could see what was going on. Kate saw a woman standing in the hall. She was waving her hands around and seemed frantic.

"The Doctors have done what they can Ms. Grant," a nurse said to the hysterical lady.

Vick was slowly walking towards the nurse and dealing with the hysterical woman.

"NO, THEY HAVEN'T!" she screamed, "If they had he would be awake right now," her anger deflating.

The woman stumbled back exhausted, hitting the wall hard.

Kate saw Vick rush over to the woman's side and caught her just as she went down. Vick helped the woman carefully settle on the floor and held her while she sobbed. Kate's heart went out to this woman. Still holding the woman Vick looked up and saw Kate. Kate could see the look of pity in his eyes. He felt sorry for this woman, just like he felt sorry for Kate.

Kate left the doorway and returned to Jordan. She sat to read the book but all she could think about was that poor woman. It triggered all her own pain and disappointment and Kate broke down into tears, something she hadn't done it quite some time. Kate knew Vick hated when she felt sorry for herself, so she decided to head home.

She told the nurse behind the counter that she was leaving and headed out to her car. Once in her car she started to cry again. The tears uncontrollable. By the time she got home, she was exhausted and climbed into bed.

While lying in bed, Kate began thinking about her priorities. She'd felt so good over the last few months, was it because she was letting go of Jordan? Had she subconsciously given up hope? Making things more complicated were her feelings for Todd. As much as she ignored them, they would still surface every once in a while. It had been months since Kate had known Jordan's love and how to love him back. She worried that she was, falling out of love with Jordan and falling in love with Todd. She fell asleep with all these thoughts on her mind.

Kate did not sleep well. She tossed and turned, fighting one nightmare and then another. At one point, she woke sweating, tears falling down her face.

Kate's sleeping mind wandered to the day of the accident and she was sitting in the passenger seat of Jordan's car. He was happy and humming along to the song on the radio. Then things got very dark. Jordan turned to Kate. "You never knew how to love me. I was a fool to think you would love me forever," his voice dark.

"No, I do, I will, I swear!" pleaded Kate.

"It's too late, I'm gone, my life wasted on you," Jordan spewed.

"No, it's not to late, It's not too late!" Kate called.

Kate could see the grill of the truck angry and colliding right into Jordan. Jordan's body was thrown into the truck by the impact, his head came to rest, blood pouring from his wounds. His eyes were open but he was not breathing, and in the dream Kate knew Jordan was dead. Kate looked down at her herself and she was fine. The impact had done nothing to her.

Kate started to scream Jordan's name, over and over.

Jordan's dead eyes piercing her heart, then he spoke one last time. "I loved you," Kate feared he didn't believe she loved him back.

Kate woke scared, and crying.

All the progress Kate had made to move forward was gone. Kate wanted nothing more then to curl up into a ball and never move. Her body became stiff and tired and couldn't go back to sleep. The dream haunting her, Jordan's dead eyes haunting her. Kate could not lie there and wait until morning. She had to call the hospital to find out if Jordan was ok.

Knowing the number by heart, she dialed and waited for a nurse to pick up.

"Long term patient care," came a familiar voice. Vick had answered.

She thought maybe she would hang up but she knew her number showed up on the phone. So, Vick knew it was her.

"Kate?" Vick asked.

"Hi, Vick, sorry to call but I had a terrible dream and just needed to hear that Jordan was okay," Kate asked, waiting for Vick to come up with some rude remark about Kate wasting his time.

"I'm sorry, you had a bad dream. I just looked in on Jordan and he remains the same, no better, no worse," Vick replied, his voice was actually kind.

"Thank you, Vick, goodnight," Kate replied.

"Try to get some sleep, goodnight," Vick said and disconnected the line.

Vick was being nice, which made Kate feel worse. If Vick felt sorry for her then her life was a mess. Kate's mind kept going back to the dream and seeing Jordan die. That was bad but Jordan thinking she didn't love him was worse. With all the good things Kate had done to get her life on track, all it took was this one dream to cause it to all crash and burn.

Chapter 21

The next few days Kate's attitude went from pessimistic to downright depressed. She barely ate, and only slept when her body forced her to. Every time she closed her eyes she dreamed of Jordan and the accident. Jordan's' words haunting her, "I loved you", past tense, it brought Kate so much pain.

Todd called her cell and land line, but Kate would not answer. After a few days of not responding Todd started to come around the house but she would not answer the door. Todd would call out, but nothing made Kate move. Kate didn't even go and see Jordan.

Even Vick came around knocking, again Kate wouldn't answer. Vick called her cell phone and land line but Kate refused to answer that too. For the first few days, Lily was around and would try to answer the door when they knocked but Kate instructed her not to answer.

"Do not answer that door," Kate said.

"They're worried. If you just spoke to them about how you're feeling I am sure they could help you," Lily returned.

"No," was all Kate said.

Lily tried to express her worry about Kate.

"Kate, I am really worried, it's not good for you to sit around all day. When was the last time you went to see Jordan?" Lily asked.

"What does it matter? He doesn't even know I am there," Kate said angrily.

"Of course, he does," Lily responded. "Kate please let me call Todd, he can help you," Lily asked Kate.

"No," Kate replied, "Lily I am going to handle my own house work from now on. Please leave your key when you are done for today," Kate told Lily.

"But," Lily tried to speak.

It was on deaf ears, Kate had walked away.

Later that day Kate went down to the kitchen and saw the key on her counter. For a moment, Kate felt bad but she didn't need someone looming over her while she was self-loathing.

Kate's voicemail filled quickly on both her cell and her landline. The text messaging however did not have a limit so she let the phone die in the top drawer of her night stand.

One evening Kate could hear Todd and Vick both creeping around the house looking for an open window. Not feeling the need for fresh air, Kate kept the windows sealed tight. Kate had no use for air at all. If she could willingly stop breathing, she would.

For days Kate just sat in the living room, in the dark. In the kitchen, in the dark and in her bedroom, in the dark. She hadn't showered or put a comb through her hair. She didn't care. Who did Kate need to impress? Certainly, not herself, she was internally disgusted.

One day there was another knock at the door, this one was hard and wasn't followed by Vick or Todd yelling. The knock came again and someone yelled "Ms. Black, I'm a police officer if you could answer the door please."

Fearing the worst, she rushed to the door, realizing just before she answered, that she looked a mess.

"Just a minute," Kate called out. She grabbed a baseball hat from the closet and a sweater that she'd thrown on the floor, God knows when. Once in order she opened the door just a crack. "Yes, officer, what can I do for you?"

"Ms. Black, you have a number of people worried about you. They say you haven't returned any of their attempts to reach you. They were worried you might be in some trouble," the officer reported.

"I see," Kate said to the officer. "Officer I am just fine. I am having a difficult time dealing with the state of my boyfriend's medical condition and just want to be left alone."

"KATE!" Todd called from across the street.

Kate backed further into the house and closed the door a little. The officer put his hand on the door to stop her from closing it all the way.

"Ms. Black, it is protocol that I come in and look around to be sure you are in no danger. If you could please open the door," the officer requested.

Kate knew that her house was a mess but stepped back and let the officer in.

The officer looked around at the state of her home, the mess contained to the kitchen and living room. The rest of the house remained clean because Kate did not use it.

"Ms. Black, are you sure you are ok?" the officer asked. "Is there anyone or any support I can get for you?" the officer offered.

"Thank you, officer, I do appreciate your concern but I just want to be alone. I need time to come to terms with things and I would like to do it without an audience. I understand my friends are worried but I really cannot think about them right now," Kate replied.

The officer nodded and headed back out the door. As the officer stepped out, Kate heard Todd yell from across the street.

"KATE PLEASE!" Todd called again.

Kate stepped back into the house closing the door until she could only see the police officer.

"May I go?" Kate asked the officer.

"Yes, Ms. Black, but please take my card. Should you need my assistance please don't hesitate to call," the officer offered and handed Kate his business card.

Kate nodded, accepted the card and closed the door locking it. She turned and leaned against the door for support and released the breath she had been holding. Jordan is fine, well, still in a coma but not dead.

Kate slid to the floor suddenly weak in the knees.

Kate heard Todd yelling at the police officer, he must have come up to the door once she closed it.

"What are you doing?" Todd yelled.

"Ms. Black has told me that she is fine and would like to be left alone," the officer replied in a calm voice.

"ALONE!" Todd yelled, "She's a mess and she needs someone to get her out of there and to get some help!" Todd 's voice escalated.

"I understand your concern, Mr. Oak, and I extended to her an offer of assistance which she refused," the officer offered to Todd.

"Extended, well, isn't that hunky dory. Well, since you offered," Todd was being very sarcastic. "Break down the door and haul her butt into the hospital," Todd demanded.

"Mr. Oak, I can only use forcible entry when I have grounds, the grounds being I believe the person or persons inside the dwelling are in danger or are a danger to themselves. I do not believe that is the case here."

Todd yelled, "You've got to be kidding me!"

And there was a loud thump on the door, it made Kate jump.

"Mr. Oak I am going to have to ask you to calm yourself and remove your person from the property or I will be left with no choice but to arrest you," the officer warned.

"Okay, okay, I'm going. KATE PLEASE CALL ME!" Todd yelled one more time.

Kate heard car ignitions starting and the sound of tires on the road.

Breathing heavily, she put her forehead to her knees and tried to calm herself. She began to think about Jordan and panic set in. What if something did happen to Jordan and Kate was not there. Here she was dreaming she'd abandoned Jordan and really that's exactly what she was doing.

Kate decided that she had to go to Jordan. She waited until it was very late and she drove to the hospital, hoping to avoid Vick and Todd. Kate walked over to the bed and sat in the chair next to him. Jordan looked the same as he always did, resting peacefully. She bowed her head resting it on his shoulder and began to cry. "I'm sorry," Kate said quietly. "I did love you, I do love you" she whispered.

Kate heard a nurse talking on the phone at her station.

"Yes, I'm telling you she is here," the nurse said into the receiver, "I'll try."

Kate, paranoid, thought the nurse had seen her come in and called either Todd or Vick. She had no idea if Vick was working tonight and wasn't about to find out. Kate was not sure why but she became very scared of seeing Vick or Todd. Kate kissed Jordan and frantically made her way through the door and into the hall. Kate turned to leave when the nurse called out her name.

"Ms. Black," she called.

Kate ignored her and began to walk quicker.

"Ms. Black, Please I need to speak with you!" the nurse said loudly.

Kate just continued out of the wing and out of the hospital. Vick never caught up with her so he must not have been here tonight. Kate turned her car towards home. She very much wanted to return to the isolation and darkness, that was the only thing that brought her comfort these days. Kate was about to turn down her street when she saw Todd's car parked in her driveway. She continued past her street, watching her rear view to see if Todd noticed her.

Why couldn't they just get the hint and leave her alone. Kate had made things clear enough for them. She drove for a little while longer, not seeing Todd behind her. It was getting late and Kate was tired of driving so she decided to get a hotel room. No one would be able to find her there. She headed to the nearest hotel and parked her car around the back of the building just in case. She did not want it to be recognized.

While checking in, the clerk eyed her suspiciously. Kate looked a mess and did not carry any bags, but once her credit card cleared he was satisfied and happily handed her a key card.

Once in the hotel room, Kate finally allowed herself to shower unfortunately the only clothes she had were the ones she was wearing. She showered with them on and then she hung them to dry. She wrapped a towel around her and went to lie on the bed.

Kate looked at the clock and saw that it was past two in the morning. She laid there just looking at the red lights of the clock and slowly drifted off to sleep. The red lights turned into the red light of the street lights. NO! NO! Wake up, not again. It was too late, the dream had its claws into Kate and wasn't letting go. Kate had to sit back and let it play out as it always did, she sat with tears falling down her face and let the dream take its course.

Chapter 22

Kate woke as she always did, crying out and tears falling down her face. She got out of bed and walked over to the window. Looking out she could see people busy with their lives, not a care in the world. She was like that once. How badly she would like to go back to that time. Kate let the curtain fall and heard something being pushed under her door. She saw a white paper, and went to retrieve it, worried someone had found her. Kate exhaled when she saw it was only her receipt.

Heading to the bathroom to dress and go home, she hoped Todd had given up and gone home. Kate signed out of her room before getting into her car and driving home. Thankfully, Todd was gone. Kate decided to park her car in the garage, that way, no one knew she had returned and headed into the house for a much-needed drink.

She found exactly what she was looking for covered in dust sitting on the wine rack. She uncorked the bottle and poured herself a glass. One glass turned into two, two into a bottle, a bottle into two. Before long Kate was stumbling around her house drinking straight from the bottle.

Kate had turned on the radio to the angriest station she could find and she began head banging and mumbling the words to the song incoherently. Kate would fall or stumble into something and she would laugh, eventually making it back into the kitchen to eat something. She needed to settle her stomach.

After eating, Kate finally fell onto the couch and was about to fall asleep when she heard a crash and the sound of falling glass. She stumbled towards the sound, listening for another clue. When she found the source of the sound she also found Todd awkwardly trying to climb through Jordan's office window.

Kate couldn't help it, she started to laugh out loud.

"I do have a front door," Kate said between laughs.

"Darn it Kate! If you'd open your front door, or answer a phone once in a while, I wouldn't have to resort to breaking and entering!" Todd said angrily finally, managing to get to his feet.

"You called the cops on me...," Kate said her words accusing but slurred.

"Are you drunk?" Todd ask, he looked at her.

"Don't judge me, I'm a mess. I get to be drunk," Kate retorted.

"Kate it's ten thirty in the morning," Todd said approaching like she was about to bolt at any moment.

"Pbbbbub, it's five o-clock somewhere," was Kate's reply.

"No Kate, I really don't think it's five o-clock anywhere," Todd replied.

He approached her one small step at a time.

All of a sudden Kate felt like she was being cornered.

"DON'T MOVE!" she yelled at Todd.

Todd halted and put his hands up in retreat. "Okay," he said putting his hands in his pockets. "Where did you go last night after leaving Jordan?" Todd asked.

"So, it was you the nurse called," Kate said pointing a finger at him accusingly.

"No, she called Vick. Vick texted me that you were there and I told him to go over to the hospital to talk to you because he lived closer. I thought just in case he missed you, I could catch you when you got home but you never came home. I waited all night," Todd told her.

"I know, I saw you in my driveway, so I went to a hotel. I showered with my clothes on," she said laughing at herself. "I was a mess," Kate admitted, "I am a mess."

Kate fell to her knees. Todd was on his knees in a heart beat wrapping his arms around her.

"It's okay Kate, I got you," Todd told her.

Kate began sobbing, her body shaking so hard she thought she'd take them both to the floor. She cried until her vision went black and she fell into darkness. It surrounded her like a warm blanket. Kate had passed out, but there was no dream. It was just black. She reveled in the silence and hoped it would go on forever, but as time went on the dream started floating towards her like a bubble on the breeze. Kate tried to run from it but her feet would not move. The closer the bubble, the bigger it got until in was on top of her and swallowed her whole. Kate fell into the passenger seat, she looked over and saw Jordan.

Kate began to cry because she knew where this was going to go. The same place it always goes. Kate sat back in the seat numb, and waited for the dream to be over.

Kate woke in her bed. Her head was pounding and she felt like she might vomit. Running for the bathroom, she hit the toilet just in the nick of time. Once the heaving stopped, Kate crawled over to the sink and pulled herself to stand. She swished some water around in her mouth, breathing slowly.

Okay so Kate remembered drinking wine, the loud music, then there was a crash. TODD! NO! He's here, she thought. Todd saw her like that last night. Mortified, Kate lowered herself to the floor and moaned.

"Is it the head or the stomach?" came a male voice, Todd's voice.

Kate looked up at him, heat rising up her neck and into her cheeks, "Seriously, Todd, why are you here? I want to be alone. I don't want anyone to see me like this," Kate said angrily.

"I'd rather see you like this than not at all. Darn it Kate, we were so worried about you that we had to call the cops!" Todd said just as angry as she did the night before.

"Yes, I recall," Kate said hissing on the s.

"Please," Todd said softly, "Let's just talk."

Kate just put her head in her hands.

"Please?" Todd said again when she didn't respond.

"Fine, let me clean up and I'll be right down," Kate said.

Todd handed her a couple of pills, "For your head," he said

Kate accepted them, thanked him and waited for him to leave. Once Todd was gone she got up off the floor and showered. Kate dressed in some sweat pants and a t-shirt and headed down the stairs her bare feet slapping on the hardwood.

She found him in the kitchen and when she entered he handed her a cup of coffee. She accepted it and took a swallow. Her stomach was still uneasy and the coffee wasn't helping. Kate headed to the sink and got a glass of cold water, holding it up to her overheated face.

"Talk," Kate commanded to Todd without turning around.

"What is going on Kate? I mean one day you're fine and the next?"

"I realized that I've abandoned the man I love," Kate answered.

"Abandoned? No, Kate, you're just moving forward. Jordan would have wanted you to," Todd soothed.

Todd repositioned himself beside Kate and put a hand on her shoulder.

Kate looked to Todd, her eyes filled with misery and pain. and her body started to tremble uncontrollably. Todd pulled her into his arms and held her tight.

"Move on. How would he have wanted me to move on?" Kate asked shakily.

Todd leaned back and looked her in the eyes, "With someone who will love you," Todd said quietly.

Kate looked away, "I will never find love again."

Todd grabbed her by the chin and forced her to look at him again. "I Love you."

"Pfft, you're my friend you have to love me," Kate made a lame attempt at a joke.

"Okay, let me rephrase. I am in love with you," Todd said, his eyes not releasing hers.

Kate said nothing, she was stunned, speechless. "What!?" she thought to herself.

Todd took advantage of her silence and leaned in and kissed her on the lips very gently.

Still in shock Kate couldn't move so Todd deepened the kiss. He started running his tongue over her lips, slowly trying to part them.

Kate was drawn in by the kiss for a moment, she wanted this. She wanted Todd but what about Jordan? She wanted him too. Todd was here and it felt good to be held like this just as she was about to return the kiss, the guilt slapped her across the face. Her brain turned back on and she jumped out of Todd's grasp.

"Oh, no! Oh no," Kate said over and over she began pacing the room. "Oh, my goodness, you're his best friend. I'm his..., You're his best friend!" growling the second-time Kate said it. "How can you think? What are you thinking!?" she yelled.

Kate couldn't stop pacing, Todd tried to approach her, to comfort her. She jumped back and put her hands up.

"OHHHH, NO, you stay right where you are," she said backing away. "Better yet, get out," Kate demanded.

"What?" asked Todd

"You heard me. Get out!" Kate said louder.

"Please Kate, let's talk about this," Todd pleaded.

"You're disloyal, you're manipulative and you have no right to call yourself Jordan's best friend. GET OUT!" Kate yelled.

Kate could tell the last part had hit a nerve.

"Fine!" Todd said heated and headed for the door. "Let the world swallow you whole, waste your life, who cares?" Todd yelled and peeled open the door.

Just as Todd did, they found Lily on the other side posed ready to knock.

"Oh, and I hired your maid back!" Todd fired his words at Kate and stormed off.

"Are you kidding me?" Kate yelled out loud.

Kate looked over at Lily who still stood there unsure of what to do.

"Do I stay or do I go?" Lily asked.

"Argh, stay," Kate replied and stormed off to her room to stew.

Chapter 23

Kate was so angry at Todd that she forgot she was wallowing in self pity and blaming herself for Jordan being in a coma. She laid in her bed playing it over and over again in her mind. When? How? Why? Why now? Why her? Kate knew that she had feelings for Todd, but she never imagined he would return them.

Kate was as angry at herself as she was at Todd. Probably angrier at herself. Todd made a good scapegoat. He loved her? Kate thought her heart becoming very heavy. Todd could have any girl why doesn't he go pick one of them.

Fuming, Kate stewed for about an hour before there came a knock at her bedroom door.

"What!?" Kate yelled at the door.

Lily slowly poked her head in, "Sorry to disturb you Kate, but I was a little concerned about the broken window? Did someone break in?" she asked.

"Argh!! Yes, Todd," Kate said angrily.

Lily nodded, not seeming surprised.

"Would you like me to call a repairman?" Lily asked.

Lily was being so nice to her after getting fired, then rehired and having to deal with a raving lunatic. Lily didn't deserve how Kate was treating her.

"No Lily, thank you, I will take care of it," Kate said changing her tone.

Lily nodded and turned to leave.

"Lily wait," Kate requested, "I am sorry for my behaviour, I am being unfair to you. I want you to know that you will still be paid for the time I had requested you to leave."

"Thank you, Kate, but you do not need to apologize to me. I can't even begin to imagine how I would behave had I been put in your situation," Lily offered.

"You're a good friend Lily" Kate replied.

"I'm still glad you call me a friend," Lily said.

Lily smiled at Kate and left. Kate felt terrible. Of course, she still thought Lily a friend. However, Kate did not feel like she was a very good one.

Kate grabbed her cell phone from the drawer and plugged it into the charger. After a few minutes the phone came to life. Once powered up it dinged, beeped and swooshed for, what felt like minutes. Kate rolled her eyes, it was all the ignored voicemails and text messages she'd gotten while her phone was off. Kate cleared her notifications and looked up a repairman.

She called a repairman and he was at her house within the hour. Kate stood with him assessing the damage.

"Baseball?" the repairman asked jokingly.

"More like dingbat," Kate retorted.

The repairman nodded in understanding and got to work. Kate could only imagine the stories this guy could tell his beer buddies. The repair guy had to leave to pick up a window but was back and had it installed by the end of the day.

Lily had finished her work and left but not before preparing a soup and sandwich, which Kate found sitting on the kitchen table. Kate frowned. Lily remained kind to Kate, which made Kate feel guilty for her actions. She'd make it up to her somehow.

Kate sat and ate a little of the soup and sandwich, her appetite was still non-existent. The low of her depression seemed to have subsided some, but not enough for Kate to see past her own misery. Kate looked over at the wine rack, which still held many bottles, and thought she could try repeating last night. Deciding it probably wasn't the best answer, she decided she would go and sit with Jordan.

Kate didn't bother changing from her jogging pants and t-shirt. She just grabbed her purse and headed out to the garage to get her car. The drive was like every other time she drove to the hospital. At the hospital, she parked and headed to the front doors. Kate walked this path so many times, that she was unaware of her surroundings. She couldn't recall the time it took her to get from her car to Jordan's wing. She rounded the corner that lead to the long-term care wing and as she passed the nurses' station, Kate hissed at the nurses.

"Do NOT call anyone," Kate warned them.

They were shocked and silenced by Kate's directness that all they could do was nod in acknowledgment. Kate walked away leaving them stunned and starring after her.

She went into Jordan's room and he was a right where she left him. Kate walked over to the bed and ran a hand over Jordan's arm.

"I miss you so much," she said. "I'm making a mess of everything."

Kate sat in the chair and just let the tears fall silently.

The nurse came in to do Jordan's vitals and while she was taking his blood pressure, Vick walked in.

Kate turned to look at the nurse accusingly. The nurse shook her head no and put her hands up.

"I swear I didn't," the nurse said.

Kate nodded, she believed her. Todd probably called Vick about the events of the past twenty-four hours and Vick was here to what? Help Todd win his girl? Or accuse Kate of being a bad girlfriend to Jordan? The latter was more likely.

Vick eyeballed Kate and then the nurse and back to Kate, raising an eye brow in question.

Kate shook her head to forget it, Vick shrugged it off.

"I came to check in on my bro here. I figured it would make you happy to know that while you were stewing in self-pity someone was still here with him," Vick said begrudgingly.

Kate felt guilty, then ashamed and then, appreciative for Vick's efforts and forethought.

"So, I guess you're here because Todd called you and told you everything?" Kate said pointing out the obvious.

Vick shook his head no.

"Haven't heard from him since yesterday when he told me he broke into your house and found you hammered out of your tree."

Again, Kate felt ashamed, why did he have to tell Vick that part. Her face began to get heated with residual anger.

"Guessing there's a story to be told. You guys have a fight?" Vick asked.

Vick must be having one of his moods swings if he actually cared.

"A fight," Kate scoffed, "Oh, you could say that!"

"Well, I feel like this is going to be good, so let me sit down first," Vick replied.

Vick sat and Kate walked him through how everything that had gone down, not sure why, but it felt good to get it off her chest, even if it was to Vick.

"Can you believe it?" Kate asked, once she was finished her story.

Vick sat still is disbelief herself.

"Wow, he finally did it," was Vick's response.

"What?" Kate asked confused.

"Oh, that boy has been lusting after you for years, but would never do anything to ruin his and Jordan's relationship," Vick told her.

"You knew?" Kate asked.

"Of course, I knew, he is my big brother, plus the boners were a dead give-away," replied Vick.

Kates opened her mouth to speak but nothing came out. The boners?

"Don't beat yourself up over it. Your home was with Jordan. Everybody else was really nice furniture," Vick said partly joking.

"Could this day get any worse?" Kate asked out loud.

Fate, deciding it wasn't quite done with her yet, dealt Kate another blow.

Whoever said lighting doesn't strike in the same place twice was a nimrod because Kate felt like a lightning rod being held up in a lightning storm, getting jolted repeatedly with no end in sight.

Chapter 24

Vick leaned back in the chair watching Kate pace the room. Wow, she is really worked up, he thought to himself. It was adorable how naive Kate was when it came to love. Kate was so cocooned in her little life with Jordan that she was so oblivious to anyone else around her. Vick had known how Todd felt about Kate since the first time he saw them in the same room.

Todd's company had a cocktail party and Todd had invited Vick and Jordan to come so he "could have people he wanted to talk to," as Todd put it. Vick had gone solo with the hopes of leaving with someone. Jordan entered with this beautiful brunette, Kate, on his arm. The entire room seemed to notice their entrance. Vick remembers the little black dress Kate wore. It was tight fitting it fell just above her knees. It was the perfect choice and she wore it well.

Jordan and Kate spent the evening in each others' eyes. Vick would have vomited had it been any other couple, but

Jordan deserved to be ridiculously happy. Vick wanted to be happy for him, had it not been Kate on his arm.

Todd however seemed quite off that night. He was usually a peacock parading around the room while girls swooned around him, all vying for Todd's attention. But Todd couldn't take his eyes off Jordan and Kate, and barely worked the room. Vick thought it was because Todd was worried about his friend. He could be very protective of Jordan but the few times Jordan left Kate's side, Todd was instantly there to take his place.

Vick noticed while talking with Kate that Todd was charming and debonair. This was very out of character. Vick knew that Todd turned on the charm when he was looking to get into some chick's pants but it shocked Vick that Todd was trying to get into Kate's.

It was close to the end of the night. When Todd, doing his bare minimum to work the room made his way over to Vick.

"Why have you been staring at me all night?" Todd asked him.

"I'm just wondering why playboy Todd is out around Jordan's girl?" Vick replied with one eyebrow raised.

"I don't know what you are talking about," Todd said sounding insulted.

"Sure," replied Vick, "Please remember I've known you my whole life."

"Seriously, Vick, I'm being nice. It's Jordan's girl," Todd said heatedly.

"Ok, if you insist," Vick replied.

Vick almost thought he should apologize to Todd for his assumptions, but later that night as the valet brought up Jordan's car, Todd and Jordan shook hands and then Kate, surprising Todd, gave him a hug good bye. Todd went beet red and quickly gave Kate a pat on the back and rushed away. Todd looked to Vick and Vick knew everything he needed to know. Vick had that look once or twice himself. It was the look of lust and pain, and it was excruciating.

Vick couldn't blame him, she did have a certain appeal. Vick should know he'd been lusting after Kate himself ever since the first time he saw her and it was a punch to the gut watching Kate walk in on Jordan's arm. It was hard seeing how happy they were together. After the hospital, Vick never thought he would ever see Kate again and he certainly did not expect to see her with his friend.

Vick doubted that Kate even remembered him from the time at the hospital when her parents passed. Jordan had introduced them and Kate had no recognition at all. Vick wasn't going to be like "Oh hey, I met you the day your parents were carted off from the morgue."

So, Vick left that cocktail party without reminding her.

Vick returned his attention to Kate. She was ranting, and then sobbing and then ranting again.

"That's it. I am done with men," Kate announced, "It's all heartbreak and getting hit by trucks."

Kate realizing what she just said covered her mouth in shock.

"Oh, my! I did not mean to say it like that," she cried.

Vick stood and pulled Kate into a hug, which was something Vick had never done before. Kate felt right in Vick arms. It was hard for Vick to be this close to Kate. Vick did his best to fill his needs and wants with other women, but sometimes he would close his eyes and think of Kate.

"I'm not sure what is happening, I mean could Todd be right? If Jordan is not coming back to me, would he want me to move on? And with his best friend?" Kate asked softly, pulling from the embrace.

"I know that Jordan wouldn't want you to be like this and he wouldn't want you to be alone," Vick replied sincerely.

"I never thought of a life without Jordan," Kate said defeated.

Vick thought, if Kate was considering Todd, then why not him? Besides the fact that she must see him as a total Jerk. Vick had to tell her the truth, then Kate would know why he was the way he was.

"Kate, I know I haven't treated you very well, and it's not that I meant to be a complete jerk. It's just that since I met you I have been drawn to you, but you were Jordan's girl. When I am around you I lose control and then hate you, and myself because I can't love you. I want you to know that you matter more to me than you know and I want you to care for me in return. If you're honestly thinking about moving on, I want you to think about moving on with me."

As he said this Vick edged closer and closer to Kate until he was standing right in front of her.

"I am also in love with you," Vick told Kate.

Vick drawing on all his courage pulled Kate into his arms and gently placed his lips to hers. Vick felt Kates body go rigid from shock, but she didn't push him away. Vick getting greedy deepened the kiss, working his tongue into Kates mouth. Kate still did not push him away. What did this mean? Vick thought to himself, could I have a shot?

Kate finally did pull out of the kiss.

"I know this is a lot for you to take in and believe me I do not want to be vying for the same girl as my bro..." Vick said.

"It must be an Oak thing," Kate said, interrupting Vick.

"What?" Vick asked

"Not understanding what truly loving someone is like, and the sheer lack of loyalty. I mean I shouldn't be too surprised you guys do come by it honestly," Kate said matter of fact.

Vick did not have many buttons but saying he was anything like his parents was the worst of all things, "How dare you!" Vick hissed.

"How Dare I?" Kate said laughing, "That's rich."

"You may want to be careful what you say next!" Vick commanded.

"Why? If the shoe fits," was Kates response.

"Because if you don't then you will be one lonely little girl," Vick replied steaming.

"I'm already lonely, you idiot. I thought I had you and Todd but apparently, you guys are out for yourselves, fool me once...." Kate trailed off.

"We have been here for you, and for Jordan, I've been there for you longer than anyone," Vick spewed.

"JORDAN!" Kate yelled "Hello, I'm WITH Jordan," Kate ranted. "And you guys suck as friends."

"Really, we watched you pine over a man who probably will never wake up and tried to help you. We watched you self-destruct and tried to help you, and oh hey, how about we watched your self centeredness, like you are the only one who cares about the man lying in that bed and still tried to help you. But news flash he's been in my life waaaayyyy longer than yours, lady. Todd and I know when it's time to say good bye," Vick screamed.

"I repeat, you suck as a friend," Kate said loudly. "Seriously! Do you think Jordan's accident was some kind of sign for you!" Kate said yelling. "Well it's not! What are you going to do now?"

Vick was so angry at Kate that the words left his mouth before he could stop them.

"I'm told life goes on, isn't that right Kate?"

Before Vick could continue a nurse rushed in and demanded they keep it down, that they were disrupting other patients in the wing. Vick huffed, glaring at Kate, who didn't even acknowledge the nurse. She just stood there with a look of confusion on her face.

Vick waited a moment to see if Kate would remember. He knew she did because, her hand fluttered to her chest and she sunk down into the chair beside Jordan's bed.

Kate dropped her face to her hands, "Get out..." she commanded.

"Do I need to call in Security?" The nurse asked.

"No," Vick said through clenched teeth, "I'm leaving, have a nice life Kate," Vick announced and stormed out of the room, vowing Kate would get hers.

Chapter 25

Kate hadn't known the nurse who had spoken to her just before she left the hospital, after her parent's death was Vick. Why wouldn't he have told her. Kate sat with her head in her hands for a while and then turned to Jordan angry at him for the first time since the accident.

"This is what you've left me with…. Nothing, absolutely nothing," Kate said angrily.

Kate didn't leave the hospital that night. She sat in the dark well into the night just running all that had happened through her mind. Eventually falling asleep in the chair. Her nightmare returned except she didn't wake this time when Jordan said the words, "I loved you."

Instead she was yanked out of the car. Holding out her arms trying to reach for Jordan as she was pulled from the car. Jordan got smaller and smaller until he disappeared. Kate found herself lying on the ground with Todd and Vick's faces floating above her. They each had a tight grip on her arms.

Todd said, "I love you, be with me."

"No, I've loved you longer, pick me," challenged Vick.

"You've destroyed the memory of us," said Jordan appearing suddenly lying beside her, his head wound still gushing.

"No," Kate said to Jordan over and over again. Meanwhile Todd and Vick kept repeating, "Pick me". They pulled at her arms until she felt like she was being torn in two, but all she could do was look at Jordan.

"Kate," she heard someone else calling her name.

"Kate," came the voice again.

Kate could feel her shoulder being shaken. It took Kate a moment to focus and realize she was waking and opened her eyes. Looking up, Kate saw Lily, who was standing before her.

Kate breathed a sigh of relief to have been pulled from the dream.

"It didn't seem like you were having a very nice dream," Lily commented.

"No," Kate agreed, "they are never very nice anymore."

Lily lifted an eyebrow questioning what Kate meant.

"I guess I'm still having a hard time with all of this," Kate said waving at Jordan on the bed. "And things just keep getting more complicated. I feel like I can hardly breathe."

"More complicated?" Lily said in horror, "is everything okay with Jordan?"

"Oh, yes. I mean, he's the same, its other things," Kate replied. "Never mind, what brings you in?"

"I like to come in and say hello when I get a chance, I miss him too," Lily said in a sad voice.

"Of course," Kate said, "I didn't mean to imply otherwise. I just can't recall you ever being here before."

"I never come in when anyone else is here, I don't want to intrude, but I overheard the nurses at shift change say something about a commotion in here and to keep an eye who is coming and going from this room. Then I looked in and saw you in obvious discomfort while you slept," Lily offered, "I may not be one of your good friends but I thought I would check in on you anyway."

"Please, I hope you don't think that. Our friendship is very important to me, I'm sorry if I haven't been such a good friend to you lately," Kate replied mortified.

"It's fine Kate, it's not like I can't understand why. But things seemed good, like you were settling. What's changed?" Lily asked.

"Everything," was all Kate could say in reply.

"Sounds like someone could use a cup of coffee and friend who can listen," Lily offered.

Kate looked to Lily who seemed to show up and be a soft place to land during all the turbulence.

"You are a good friend, Lily, coffee would be perfect," Kate replied. She stood and began walking out the door.

However, before Lily left she went over to Jordan's bed and placed a hand on his arm, "come back soon," Lily said and headed out the door.

Kate was struck by Lily's hope that Jordan would return, Kate used to have hope but somehow, she'd lost that. Standing here, Kate returned to her convictions. Jordan was coming back. Screw everyone else and what they thought.

Kate and Lily went to a little coffee shop around the corner from the hospital. Lily insisted Kate eat something other then the food at the hospital cafeteria. She didn't feel much like eating but agreed to get out of the hospital for a moment. Once at the shop they ordered and sat with two steaming hot cups of coffee and a bagel for Kate, which she set aside.

Kate began to tell Lily what had happened, beginning from when Todd had broken into her house finishing with the fight with Vick last night. Lily sat quietly listening nodding at times urging Kate to continue.

"Can you believe it?" Kate asked Lily once she finished her tale.

"Oh, Kate, the heart wants what the heart wants," Lily replied, "It's a difficult position for you for sure, but I get why they did it."

"Really?" Kate asked absolutely dumbfounded.

"Yes. When you find you're in love with someone it's amazing, but to have to keep it to yourself is like being punched in the gut over and over with no end in sight. After all that pain, all you can think of is there needs to be a better way, and then life throws you an opportunity to fight back, and you think 'I might win'. Who wouldn't take the chance to be rid of all that pain?" Lily explained.

"Why does it seem like you're talking from experience?" Kate asked.

Lily looked up at Kate and saw had a look on her face Kate had seen before. Todd had that look and Vick had that look. Oh no! She thought not you too.

"Please Lily, not you too. I can't take another proclamation of someone's love for me!" Kate said horrified.

Lily laughed, "I do love you Kate, but my proclamation would not be for you. I mean, your cute and all, but really not my type," Lily said laughter hanging on her every word.

"Thank goodness," Kate said relieved and then mortified at how self-centered she sounded. "I'm sorry, that I jumped to that conclusion, but who is your proclamation for?" Kate asked.

"It doesn't matter, he's made his love known to another," Lily said not realizing that she nodded at Kate when she said it.

Kate knew that whoever Lily loved had said they loved Kate, and since Lily said he, it had to be Jordan, Todd or Vick.

Lily did say she only came to see Jordan when she could visit with him alone.

"Jordan?" Kate asked quietly afraid of the answer.

Lily looking shocked, possibly because Kate had figured it out.

"No," Lily said to Kate, "Not Jordan," in a very quiet voice. Lily confessed the name of the man she loved, "Todd."

Kate stunned, thought how this web kept getting bigger and bigger. They sat silent for a while, exchanging smaller pleasantries before Lily announced she had to get to work. Lily had many clients she worked for. Kate nodded and sat a while longer before getting up.

Heading out onto the sidewalk, Kate began the walk back to the hospital. She was deep in thought and did not look both ways when she crossed the street. Kate heard someone scream in horror and she realized too late, why.

Kate didn't see the car until it was too late, it all happened very slow. She could hear the screaming of other pedestrians on the street, but they were dulled by the sound of the screeching tires of the car trying to brake. Kate felt the impact of the car and felt herself hitting the hood of the car. She heard the crack of her head hitting the windshield and just as she was about to feel the pain of it all, her world went black.

Chapter 26

It was pitch black where Kate was but she could hear the commotion of the people around her.

"Hold on!" someone cried out, "an ambulance is on it's way."

"Oh, my God, oh my God," another person kept saying obviously in shock from witnessing what had just happened.

Kate heard a siren in the distance, maybe it was the ambulance.

It was funny but Kate didn't feel panicked, she was calm. There was a dull ache of pain but it was bearable. Perhaps her injuries were not that bad. Then why couldn't she open her eyes, Kate thought.

"Ma'am, ma'am," but the voice was different.

Kate felt hands on her neck and then something was wrapped around it. She was rolled to one side and then on her back again. Then Kate felt like she was floating through the air. Doors slammed and the sirens were wailing again.

It felt like seconds before Kate heard more voices, one commanding voice and others faded.

"Run her name and find out her next of kin," said the commanding voice.

"Yes, Doctor," said another.

Kate heard the bustling, felt the hands on her body. The doctor must be checking her for injury, Kate thought.

"Doctor, we have a problem," said a voice, "the next of kin listed is currently in a coma in the Long-Term Care wing here at the hospital.

"What is this Patient's name?" asked another voice.

"Kate Black," the first voice replied.

There was a pause, "I know who to call," said the second voice.

The dull ache of Kate's body started to become more intense and before she knew it, she was opening her eyes. The pain in her head was unbearable, she cried out in pain.

The doctor turned his attention to her.

"Ms. Black" he called. "Can you hear me?" he asked.

"My head, it hurts so bad!" Kate cried.

"Can you follow my finger?" the doctor asked placing a finger in front of Kate's face.

Kate looked past the doctor's fingers at the lights in the ceiling, why did she see red veins on them, she looked to the doctor and there was red on him. She couldn't concentrate on anything; the pain was pulsing in her head.

"Ms. Black, please can you hear me?" the doctor asked again.

Kate couldn't bear it any longer and her vision began to blur, it went bright white and then faded into black but this time the voices drifted off until there was only silence and the pain was gone.

* * * * * *

Vick got the call from the nurse at the hospital.

"No!" Vick yelled into his phone. "I'm on my way."

Vick was really angry with Kate, he said and thought things out of anger but he did not want anything bad to happen to Kate.

Vick grabbed his wallet as he was running out the door, texting Todd the news as he ran to his car.

Vick jumped into his car, started the ignition and paused just for a second to catch his breath. Once he knew he wasn't going to hyperventilate he slammed the car in drive and was off like a shot.

* * * * * *

Todd was lying in bed with his Kate look-alike sleeping at his side when he heard the ding of a text message coming in. He reached for the phone to see who it was.

He read the message and jumped out of bed, "No, oh no! No!" Todd shouted.

Todd ran around the room trying to dress as quickly as he could.

"What is it? You look like someone is about to die" Kate's look alike said.

Todd stopped short in his tracks.

"You better hope not," he said and headed for the door.

"Let yourself out," Todd commanded as he ran for his car.

The elevator took much longer then it usually did, Todd tapped his foot impatiently. Getting so frustrated at the length of time he punched the wall, his hand going straight through and connecting with concrete. Todd cried out in pain, looking at his hand, that instantly started to swell.

The elevator dinged and the doors opened Todd jumped in hoping nobody else would be getting on. Luckily for him, and them, no one did. He ran to his car in the garage and squealed his tires as he raced out of the cement structure, driving with only one hand.

* * * * * *

Lily had to run a few errands before she went to work and decided to take care of them while she was by the hospital. She had made it to only one shop, when she came out and saw that there was a commotion up the street. Her car was that way so she headed there to see what was going on.

Once Lily got to the scene she started to yell in a panic "Oh my goodness," she said repeatedly, Lily just stood there in utter shock, while Kate was lying on the ground being attended to. The EMS workers came and Kate was quickly rushed to the hospital.

Lily dropped her bags and ran as fast as she could so she could get to the ER. Kate was already unloaded and being treated when Lily got there. She ran up to the nurse's station and asked about Kate, the nurse asked if Lily was family.

"No, she doesn't have any family!" Lily yelled, "she is my friend and employer."

"I'm sorry Miss but I can only speak to family or next of kin," the nurse said.

"It's alright Kim," said another nurse who had just approached, "I can handle this."

Kim nodded and left.

"I have already put a call into Vick, once Vick arrives and can corroborate who you are, then I can tell you more about Ms. Black's condition," the nurse told her.

Lily nodded and went to wait for Vick to arrive.

Lily jumped to her feet when she heard a scream. Lily knew it was Kate and didn't take her eyes off Kate's room. Within minutes Kate was being rushed out and away.

"Where are they going? Where are they taking Kate?" Lily demanded hysterically.

"To surgery," the nurse replied.

"Surgery," Lily saying the word, as though it was foreign and didn't belong.

Lily sank back into her chair worried about her friend.

It may have been minutes, it could have been hours, time ceased for Lily. Vick finally came rushing through the doors of the ER and she jumped to her feet to greet him.

Vick looked at her confused,

"Lily what are you doing here?" Vick asked.

"I was having coffee with Kate this morning, I mean I wasn't with her when it happened but I was shortly before and then I saw ….," Lily trailed off

Vick shrugged uncaring and headed to the nurse's station.

"How is she? Where is she?" Vick asked the nurse behind the station.

The Nurse nodded towards Lily, silently asking if she could speak in front of her.

"Yes, yes, just tell me," Vick replied hastily.

"She sustained a severe head injury, and the doctor suspects some broken ribs. They're worried about the possibility of a punctured lung, so she was taken for scans and then likely into surgery," the nurse informed them.

"Who is the doctor on call?" Vick asked

"Dr. Roberts," replied the nurse with a grimace.

"Darn it!" Vick said.

"What? Why?" Lilly asked worried at the concern Vick had over the doctor treating Kate.

"Oh, sorry I didn't mean to worry you. Dr. Roberts is a good doctor. It's just he's doesn't believe in giving special treatment to people who work here. So, I won't be able to call the operating room for updates. We have to wait and see like any normal family member," Vick replied.

Just then Todd rushed into the emergency room. Todd hurried up to Vick, giving Lily the once over but otherwise ignoring her.

"Tell me?" Todd asked Vick.

Vick brought Todd up to speed, finishing with the unfortunate wait and see.

"Darn it!" Todd replied to that, heading to the private waiting room with Lily ambling behind.

It was hard for Lily to sit and not do something comforting for Todd, but he barely noticed her presence. Lily stayed to herself and remained quiet, just waiting for news on Kate's condition.

Chapter 27

Kate liked the darkness. It was comforting and calm. She felt no confusion here, no pain. She wanted to stay in the safety of the darkness.

Kate saw some movement in the darkness, then a hand was pulling back the darkness like a curtain made of steel. She could see the person was struggling to get through, and they finally made it. Once the figure was on the other side of the curtain it fell and all was black again. Kate was no longer alone. The figure approached and it was herself, except she was wearing clothes straight out of the 1800's.

Great, this dream again, Kate thought to herself.

"Man, you're strong," the look-alike yelled to the darkness, "but I am stronger."

The look-alike turned, "Well, I cannot believe we are finally standing face to face and able to talk," she acknowledged.

Kate just stood there shocked. What in the heck was her mind doing to her?

"Great," the look-alike said, "you can't hear me, again. This is next to impossible," she said looking up.

Who was she talking to? Kate wondered.

"I can hear you," Kate said

The look-alike was startled, looked to Kate, "Thank goodness, I might finally have a shot here."

The look-alike rushed to be right in front of Kate.

"My name is Katherine. I have been trying to reach you, or another me, forever. I thought I had finally managed with that medium but you did nothing with what she told you."

Kate had to think for a minute, what was she talking about? What medium? Then it came to her. The woman from the farmer's market.

"My mind sure is messing with me right now," Kate said aloud.

Katherine put her hand to her head in defeat.

"How am I going to convince her? Of course, this is hard to believe," Katherine said.

Katherine turned and spoke to someone behind her.

"I know it's the only way but, what do I say?" she asked.

Kate looked behind Katherine but all she saw was darkness.

"Kate!" called a voice through the darkness, it sounded like Jordan.

Kate perked up and started running towards the sound. Jordan called out again, it was him.

Kate hit the darkness, it felt like a cement wall. She pushed and pushed with all her might until it slowly started to give. Finally, the darkness parted and Kate stepped into white, blinding light.

Kate's eyes adjusted and she saw him. Jordan was standing in what looked like a glass box. It was exactly like the other dream she had a few months back, during her unfortunate incident in the tub. Katherine stepped into the white just as Kate ran to Jordan.

Kate put her hand to the glass.

"Jordan," she said, happy to see him and able to speak to him.

"Hi baby," Jordan said to her.

Katherine had joined them at the glass.

"So, what do we say to her that will make her believe what we are telling her is real and not in her head," Katherine asked.

"I could tell her something only she and I would know," Jordan offered not taking his eyes off Kate.

"She thinks her mind is playing tricks on her so if she knows it, then it can be from her mind and not you," said the other man standing in the glass prison with Jordan.

Kate remembered him from her dream, he looks just like Jordan but there was a difference she couldn't put her finger on.

"Right," said Jordan this time looking to Katherine.

Jordan was silent for a moment and then looked up to Kate.

"I've got it," he said looking pleased with himself.

"Kate, did you get my personal effects from the hospital after the accident?" Jordan asked.

Kate nodded yes.

"Did you look at what was there?" Jordan asked

Kate shook her head no.

Jordan looking very happy with the answer.

Said, "Good, when you wake,"

"If she wakes," said the man in the prison with Jordan, interrupting, pointing his finger to the ceiling.

The darkness was falling just like it did in Kate's other dream.

Jordan began to talk quickly.

"When you wake," he insisted, "in the bag of stuff there is a ring box, and it holds a solitaire diamond ring, with the inscription, 'Baby, I will take you with me.'

Kate began to tear, she just wanted to be in his arms, what is with the glass prison?

"Why are you in there and who is this guy?" Kate asked.

"I am trapped in here so that I cannot come back to you," Jordan said quietly.

"And that man, is John, he is my Jordan, also caged so that we cannot be together," Katherine offered.

"Why are you doing this?" Kate demanded angrily, looking at Katherine.

Katherine shrugged her shoulders.

"I don't know, but if you fix it we can all be free," Katherine replied.

"Just stop it!" Kate yelled.

"I've tried Kate, I swear I have tried, I don't know how this works I just know how to end it," Katherine replied sadly. "We do not have much time Kate. Do you see that darkness?"

Kate nodded.

"That's not the way back, that's the way home," Katherine told her.

Kate was confused, what did that mean?

As if she knew Kate was confused.

"That's my Victor, so in other words, that's death," Katherine said loudly.

Kate for some reason knew this to be true and began to panic, she didn't want to die but she didn't know how to get away from it.

"I don't know what to do?" Kate asked as a question to the others.

Katherine shrugged her shoulders walking towards Kate.

"I'm not really sure either, but we could do what we did last time, that seemed to work," Katherine said.

Kate still confused.

"What did we do last time?" she asked.

Katherine lifted a hand in the air and smacked Kate hard across the face. There was an explosion of colour and when she refocussed her eyes she saw the worried faces of Vick, Todd and Lily.

"Kate," Todd said leaping to his feet.

"Well, she's alive, great!" Vick said sarcastically and then left the room.

It didn't take long for Kate to focus on what had happened and Kate recalled her dream. It was too real, she had to be sure one way or another.

"Lily," Kate said ignoring Todd. "On Jordan's desk is a hospital bag. It has whatever Jordan had on his person after the accident. Can you please go and get it for me right now?" Kate said frantically.

"Kate, I'm sure there are more important things right now?" Todd said.

"No, Todd, there isn't," Kate said sternly.

"It's fine Todd, I'm happy to do whatever Kate needs," Lily smiled and left the room.

Todd came over to Kate's bedside. She could see how worried he was. She could see his love for her in his eyes. Kate could not deal with that right now.

"Todd, I'd like to be alone for now," she told him.

Kate knew Todd was shocked and upset that she would send him away but he did not argue with her. He just shook his head and slowly sauntered out of the room with his head bowed.

Kate felt terrible about sending Todd away and she knew at some point Kate would have to figure things out, but right now all she could think about was that dream and how badly she wanted it to be true.

Now that Kate was alone all she could do was wait, wait and see if Jordan really needed help to come back to her, or that she had completely lost her mind. Either way as long as Jordan was where she ended up Kate didn't care.

Chapter 28

While Lily was on her errand to gather Jordan's personal belongings, Kate's doctor came in to examine her. She was irritated, she just wanted to be left alone. Kate tried to concentrate on what he was saying in an attempt to distract herself from what may or may not be in that bag of Jordan's.

"You're one lucky lady," said the doctor, while he was pointing a light into her eyes.

"How do you figure?" Kate asked the doctor sarcastically.

"Well, besides the trauma to the brain, there were no other severe injuries. With an accident like that, you're lucky to be alive," he explained.

"I suppose!" Kate replied, cynically.

The doctor gave her a questionable look.

"You don't think you're lucky to be alive?" He questioned.

"It's not that. Of course, I'm happy to be alive, but my boyfriend is on another floor in a coma and I don't know if he will ever wake," Kate replied, "So I'm not overjoyed at the idea of a life without him."

"I see," was all the doctor said.

The doctor walked Kate through all her injuries and what she needed to do next in order to heal and go home.

Apparently, she had sustained a very bad head injury. Her brain had swollen they did what they could but were not sure their efforts would be enough. Thankfully the brain swelling began to subside. The doctor told her that it had been three days since Kate was struck by the car and that she was sedated the whole time. They had stopped the sedation once her brain swelling went down and waited for her to wake.

Just like Jordan, except she woke up, Kate thought.

Aside from some bruised ribs, she did not sustain any other injuries. The doctor was satisfied with how she was doing and said he would be back to check on her later. Kate nodded and the doctor left.

Kate was getting impatient waiting for Lily to return. She sat back to rest her eyes and ended up falling into a light sleep. Kate could still hear what was going on around her, and jerked to a seated position, when Lily returned.

"Sorry, I had to go home for my key first," Lily explained.

Lily held Jordan's hospital bag in her hands. Kate reached for the bag and Lily handed it to her.

"Right, here you go," Lily said as she released it.

Kate held the bag for a minute. Once she opened it all her hopes could be washed away, but Kate had to know one way or another.

"Lily can I have some time alone please?" Kate asked.

"Of course, I'll come by tomorrow," Lily said.

She turned and left.

Kate's head got very dizzy, her vision blurred and her head began to hurt. Kate thought, maybe she should wait until she was healed a little more. No! Kate couldn't wait she had to know right now. Kate brought her bed to a seated position to see if that would help. She waited for the dizziness to subside. It did. Her vision cleared, but her headache did not let up. Ignoring the pain, Kate dumped the contents of the bag on her bed.

There was Jordan's clothing covered in blood, Kate's heart retracted for a second, she hated thinking about how much pain he was in that day. She picked up his shirt and put it to her nose. It still smelled like him, which was comforting. She set the shirt aside. The bag had his watch, his wallet, and a ring that belonged to his father. Kate continued to move the clothing aside and then there it was. The red ring box.

Kate's heart began to pound so hard that it might burst right out of her chest. Okay she thought, trying to reason with herself, maybe she saw the ring box without realizing and it was manifested in her dream.

Kate lifted the ring box slowly. She took a deep breath and opened it.

"Oh, my goodness!" Kate said out loud.

There it was a diamond solitaire ring. She pulled it out of the box and looked for an inscription on the inside of the band. Kate began to sob, there it was, 'Baby, I will take you with me.' It was the way her parents said I love you, and because Jordan loved her parents like they were his own, it meant the same thing to him that it did to her.

"Baby, I'll be by your side," Kate said to the empty room and cried uncontrollably for a while. The tears finally subsided and Kate was able to think about everything that had happened.

Ok, so the medium had really been seeing this spirit named Katherine. Kate never really believed in ghosts and other supernatural stuff, she wasn't even sure if she believed in God, but how else was Kate going to explain this.

Kate had no idea the ring was in the bag, let alone what the inscription would say. This was crazy, right? She asked herself. She debated telling someone to see if they could be more objective, but who? Kate had sent everyone away. Even if they were here she doubted they were even still talking to her.

Okay, so for a second, let's say it is true, she thought. The medium said that Kate would have to fix the relationship with the Victor in her time.

"What am I supposed to do?" Kate asked the empty room.

Kate thought hard about the conversation she had with the medium, still thinking it was a hoax. The medium said that Kate had to fix the relationship with the Victor of her time. The Victor of her time had to be Vick, but how does she fix a relationship that was never there.

Kate's brain hurt from trying to figure this all out which was ironic because her brain actually hurt. A nurse came in with a tray of food.

Kate had completely lost track of time, not knowing if lunch or dinner was coming next.

"Dinner's here!" announced the nurse.

Well, that solves that, maybe this nurse had the answer to her boyfriend dilemma.

The nurse went about watching the numbers on her machines, checking Kate's blood pressure, her temperature and her bandage. The nurse yammered on about recent events happening in the outside world.

"You are one lucky lady," the nurse said.

"So, I am told," Kate said sarcastically.

The nurse ignored her tone.

"I know if I had an accident like yours, I would take a serious look at my life. Maybe go and find the one that got away," the nurse admitted.

Kate rolled her eyes, that would be impossible because the one did not get away. He's in a coma and Kate couldn't get to him.

The nurse continued talking incessantly.

"There's that young man who is always calling and checking in on you. He's stopped by a couple of times but you were sleeping, he sure looks like he's more than a friend, and cute!" she said, giving Kate a wink.

"What young man?" Kate asked, who could the nurse possibly be talking about?

"Tall, dark hair," the nurse replied.

Did she mean Vick or Todd? "Was his name Vick? Is he a nurse here?" Kate asked the nurse.

The nurse thought for a moment, "Oh, I am new here, I wouldn't know dear," she said.

Kate suspected it was Vick, he had to be the one Katherine was talking about, the Victor of her time. Vick was a jerk, like Victor, and in love with Kate like Victor was with Katherine. How was Kate going to fix things with Vick? What was there to fix? Plus, Kate had sent Vick running.

She decided she had to try to fix things. She grabbed her bag of belongings from the stand beside her bed and dug around the bag until she found her cell phone. It was dead. She reached over to the hospital phone to dial Vick's number. The phone rang until the voicemail picked up. Kate wasn't sure if she should leave a message or call back. Vick was probably ignoring her calls. It was probably best to leave a message.

"Vick, its Kate. I'm sorry. We need to talk," Kate said into the phone and hung up. Hopefully he would call back, if not, she would fill his phone with messages until he did.

Kate was pretty tired and decided to close her eyes and rest. She dozed off to sleep and for the first time in a long time she dreamt of Jordan like he was, happy, energetic and in love with her.

Chapter 29

$\mathcal{K}$ate woke rested with a smile on her face. It was so nice to wake from a nice dream.

"Good dream?" asked a disgruntle voice.

Kate knew that voice, it was Vick. Kate sat up quickly, causing her head to spin, almost falling back to the bed. Vick jumped up to catch her, but she managed to hold herself up. She raised the bed so she could lean against it while she sat.

"Vick," Kate paused, "thank you for coming. I wasn't sure you would."

Kate looked down at her hands, trying to figure out what it was she wanted to say next.

"You have been part of Jordan's life since the two of you were boys. You were, sorry, are, family. I came along and everything changed," Kate began. "I had no idea of your feelings, and I am sorry for hurting you. I really suck at

220

handling difficult situations, and rather than deal with them head on I retaliate and throw hissy fits," Kate began, "I was out of line," Kate said looking at Vick.

Vick huffed while raising an eyebrow up at her questionably.

"Okay, way out of line," Kate admitted.

Vick, seemed happier with this statement and sat back in his chair.

"Vick, you are nothing like your parents, well, you have your dad's hair, which is a good thing because balding men…." Kate trailed off trying to add some humour.

Vick ran his hands through his hair and smirked.

"You have shown me kindness and consideration even though it pained you. I know I could have handled things so much better than I did and I'm sorry," Kate finished.

"Great, you've apologized, feel better?" Vick asked sarcastically. "Yes?" Vick said not waiting for a response, "great I'll go know," Vick stood to leave.

Vick sure could hold a grudge. Kate had to think of something that would make him forgive her.

Recalling the story of Katherine, being in a love triangle with John and Victor, maybe the only way to fix things was if Katherine ended up with Victor, or in Kate's case Vick. If it meant bringing Jordan back, she could sacrifice her own happiness. Kate would give anything if it meant that Jordan might live. Kate just hoped Jordan would understand why she had moved on. She hoped Jordan would not throw them all out of his life, but if that's what it takes for Jordan to live then Kate had no choice.

"What if I told you I would try to move on, and what if I said I would do that with you?" Kate asked quickly.

Vicky stopped dead in his tracks narrowed his eyes and peered at Kate. "Then I'd say prove it," Vick said challenging.

Kate thought about how she was going to prove it. There was only one thing she could think of.

"Okay, come here and sit with me," Kate asked Vick.

Vick walked over and sat down waiting for whatever Kate was going to do to prove that she wanted to be with him. Kate wrapped her arms around Vick and planted her lips on his. Vick was still at first but then he melted into the kiss. Kate willingly allowed Vick to invade her mouth and heard his moan while he pulled Kate against his body. Kate could hardly breathe but did not pull away.

Vick was the first one to pull out of the embrace and he wiped his mouth.

"You're such a liar," he said. "You don't want me."

Kate was surprised and worried that he would be angry with her.

"Yes, Vick I do," Kate began.

"Stop, I'm no fool, don't treat me like one," Vick said.

"I'm sorry," Kate said feeling very ashamed, "I'm not trying to treat you like a fool, I can't lose you. I do care for you Vick, I'm just not in love with you," Kate replied.

Vick sat there looking Kate in the eyes and thought for a moment.

"Then why say you want me? Why the kiss?" Vick asked.

"You would never believe me, if I told you the truth. All I can say is I'm trying to save us all and I'm flying by the seat of my pants and well, I'm just crashing and burning," Kate replied.

Vick was quiet for a while then he asked quietly, "you're always going to be with Jordan, aren't you?"

"Yes, Vick, I think I will," Kate responded. "I don't want to hurt you or cause you pain, but my heart and soul are tied to Jordan's endlessly."

"You don't really think I am anything like my parents," Vick asked self-consciously.

"NO!" Kate said with enthusiasm. "Vick, you're the exact opposite, someone some day is going to be one lucky gal, because you will love them and have so much to offer them."

Vick nodded, "Okay, say it one more time," he said.

Kate confused asked, "Say what?"

"Say you're sorry one more time," Vick commanded.

Kate obliged, "Vick, I am very sorry for…"

"You're forgiven!" Vick interrupted and threw his arms around Kate, "but if you ever change you mind," Vick said and winked at her and laughed.

Kate laughed too. It felt good to be in a better place with him.

Kate never dreamed that she and Vick would be friends, but in this moment, it seemed very possible.

The moment was interrupted by Vick's cell phone ringing. He pulled it out and answered it quickly.

"Yes," Vick answered, "When?" he asked sounding distraught. "I'll be right there."

Then he stuffed the phone into his pocket.

Vick stood quickly, he began looking around like he needed something but wasn't quite sure what. Kate could see the panic on his face.

"Emergency?" Kate asked leaning back and closing her eyes.

"Sort of," Vick replied.

The way he said that made Kate open her eyes. Vick was looking at Kate and the way his face looked made Kate's heart start to race.

"What is it?" she asked Vick.

"Jordan's heart stopped," Vick told her, point blank.

Kate froze, a scream caught in her throat.

"They managed to resuscitate him," Vick said, "but the doc is worried his condition is deteriorating," he told her.

Kate let out the breath she'd been holding. Jordan was alive. But his heart had stopped, he came close to death and she was here and not with him.

Then Kate remembered the medium. She had fixed the relationship with Vick. Kate didn't understand, if she and Vick were good then why is Jordan getting worse. Shouldn't he be set free now, shouldn't he be waking and coming back to Kate? Was Vick faking?

No, Vick was not faking. Kate could tell by how Vick was being with her. He was comfortable, and soft, and kind, all things Vick had never been before. Kate couldn't waste anymore time here. She had to get to Jordan.

"I need to see him Vick," Kate said.

"I don't know if you're in any condition to," Vick replied.

"Vick!" Kate yelled at him. "Take me to him."

"Okay, I'll go talk to the nurse," Vick said backing out of the room.

When Vick returned, he brought the nurse with him.

"Ms. Black," the nurse began, "you are in no condition to be out of that bed. The doctor is still not completely satisfied with your progress enough to discharge you."

"I need to get to my boyfriend!" Kate said frantically.

"I understand that Ms. Black but you will be of no use to him if you're unconscious on the floor," the nurse said in an authoritative voice.

"He's getting worse. I have to be with him," Kate pleaded.

"I will have the doctor come in and he can decide if you're able to leave the wing," the nurse said to Kate.

Kate was getting very angry and this nurse was pissing her off. If she waited for the doctor it could be too late. Kate was not going to sit here and wait for a doctor while the love of her life was fighting for his life in another room.

"Get me a wheelchair, so that I can go to my boyfriend's room," Kate growled at the nurse. "Or I will sign myself out and risk the chance of lying unconscious on the floor, as you put it. Your choice," Kate said angrily.

The nurse huffed, "Fine, why listen to a medical professional?"

The nurse stomped out of the room but returned a few minutes later with a wheelchair.

"You may want to consider keeping it brief and coming back to rest, but you do what you want," the nurse said bitterly.

The nurse left the room, not offering any help to get Kate into the chair. It was a good thing Vick was here because Kate wasn't sure she would have been able to do it on her own.

Vick helped Kate into the chair and the two of them were off to Jordan's room, as fast as Vick could push her without losing control of the chair. Kate just prayed they would make it there in time.

Chapter 30

$\mathcal{K}$ate sat with Jordan, while Vick went to get the doctor so they could figure out what was going on and what they could do to help Jordan.

Kate reached out and took Jordan's hand.

"I don't understand, I thought fixing things with Vick would set you free?" Kate asked. "Maybe I am going crazy, maybe it was just a dream and I'm trying to make it more then it was. Jordan, I just don't know," Kate said starting to sob. "Please, baby I can't bear the thought of losing you."

Vick walked back into the room.

"Doc's going to be a minute. He's in surgery," Vick said as he kicked the bed leg. "What if this is karma?" Vick asked.

"What do you mean?" Kate questioned.

"I mean, what if this is the universe's way of getting back at me and Todd for trying to take his girl," Vick replied.

"Vick, I don't know what I believe when it comes to karma but I do know this, you were not trying to "take Jordan's girl" as you say, you were trying to move on with your life after a tragedy. Like someone told me once, the heart wants what the heart wants, so I don't think this has anything to do with your karma," Kate said trying to reassure Vick.

However, it may have something to do with my karma a few times removed, Kate thought to herself.

They both sat quietly, listening to Jordan's machines and Vick's cell phone alert, letting him know that he had a message. Kate kept looking to him with every ding, getting irritated.

"Do you need to be somewhere?" Kate asked nodding at the phone.

"No. It's Todd checking in, looking for an update on Jordan," Vick informed her.

"Why doesn't he just come in? Is he working or something?" Kate asked.

"No," Vick said very quietly, "Todd's not happy with you and refuses to be where you are. That and booting him out of your room after you just woke up from a three-day coma did not help either."

Kate was taken aback. She gets that she said and did some hurtful things, but was it so bad that he would not even be in the same room with her, while his best friend was fighting for his life. Kate thought back to their argument. She knew she went too far, but she couldn't handle all that she felt when Todd kissed her. Yes, Kate did take her anger out on Todd, but she did not realize how badly she hurt him.

Kate used the phone in Jordan's room and dialed Todd's number, but it went to voicemail. Kate left the same message she had for Vick and then waited for him to call her back.

The doctor came in and apologized for being so long, explaining that surgery can take longer then expected.

Kate and Vick both nodded in understanding to the doctor and waited for him to continue.

"So, I have reviewed his charts, and scans and according to them just before Mr. Best required resuscitation, his brain function had increased higher then we have seen it," the doctor began. "All I can conclude was that this caused a lot of stress on the heart causing it to stop. His brain function has returned to what has been his normal for the last several months and he remains stable at this time," the doctor finished, looking to Kate then Vick to see if they had any questions.

"So, if his brain function went up, is that not a good sign that he's trying to wake? That it's only a mater of time?" Kate asked hopefully.

"Ms. Black the brain is such a mysterious organ, we still know very little about it, so I cannot say yes or no to that question. I'm sorry but it's just going to be more waiting and seeing if Mr. Best will wake or not," the doctor replied apologetically.

"So, is there anything we can do?" asked Vick.

"Just keep doing what you're doing, talking to him, reading to him," the doctor said nodding to Kate." "And keep hope."

The doctor's pager went off.

"I'm sorry but I do have to go. Please if there are anymore questions I will find time tomorrow to answer them," he said as he rushed out the door.

"I can't sit here right now Kate, I have to go. I'll come by in the morning to see you guys," Vick said looking uneasy, "I will have a nurse take you back to your room in a little while."

Then he left.

Kate just sat running through everything about her dream, or vision, whatever it was. The words of the medium, and the doctor's words, having hope. It wasn't long before a nurse came in and insisted that Kate go back to her room.

Over the next few days Kate spent as much time in Jordan's room as she could. She found herself getting stronger and finally to the point that she didn't even need the wheelchair. It had been a few days since Jordan's heart stopped and had to be restarted, and Kate was lying in bed trying to sleep. Kate fretted, that Jordan's heart would stop again.

Kate finally fell into a light sleeping trance and she dreamt about Katherine and Jordan in the glass prison. It wasn't like the other times. They were almost like apparitions and not real, they didn't talk to her or even acknowledge her. Kate sat crossed legged on grass, the medium, Ashley, appeared beside her.

Ashley looked around.

"Well, this is new, didn't know I could dream walk," Ashley said. "Okay, okay, I'll get to the point," she said to someone off in the distance.

Kate looked but didn't see anyone.

"I am told to tell you to remember that you have to fix the relationship with the Victor of your time," Ashley said.

"Yes, I know and I did but nothing happened aside from Jordan almost dying," Kate returned.

"No, Kate you didn't," the medium said and then just disappeared.

Kate woke, slowly opening her eyes. Why did this have to be so darn hard. Did she not fix the relationship with Vick? He seemed okay she thought, but maybe he was acting? Kate sat back in thought.

"Fix the relationship with the Victor of her time…" and then Kate realized what she did wrong. She assumed the person was Vick because of their behaviours, but there was another person in love with her, who could also be possessive and needy, like Victor was.

"Todd," Kate said.

Kate was so certain about Todd and she knew what she had to do but Todd wasn't returning her calls. Kate looked over at the clock, it was one o-clock in the morning. Todd had to be at home now.

Kate paced the hospital room floor and thought about what to do. She couldn't wait until morning to go to Todd. Her car was still here, if it didn't get towed while she was stuck in the hospital.

Kate went to the nurses' desk and looked at the nurse on duty.

"I'm leaving," she said and headed to her room to get dressed. Thankfully, Lily had brought her a few things and Kate didn't have to wear a hospital gown out in public. Kate dressed and wrapped her head in a scarf. The nurse was fretting behind Kate, telling her what a bad idea it was, that she should wait until morning.

"You are in no condition to drive," the nurse stated.

"Ok, so, you may have a point about driving. I'll call a cab," Kate offered.

The nurse sighed, frustrated, and walked out of the room.

Before long Kate was at the curb waiting for the cab she'd called. She jumped in, gave the directions to the driver and they were off. It took forty-five minutes to get to Todd's apartment. She jumped out, thanked the driver, and headed to the front doors of the building complex.

Kate hoped the concierge was at his desk but no luck. The doors were locked and the concierge was no where to be seen. Kate wasn't sure if Todd would allow her in if she called up to his apartment. Her options were to take the risk of being turned away or wait for someone to open the door.

While Kate was debating her options, a group of people walked up, not one of them walking straight. They were laughing and pushing each other, one guy fumbling with his keys trying to open the door, managing after about the third attempt.

"Open sesame!" he called out to the group and they all cheered.

They all headed through the door and Kate passed through with them.

Kate headed to the elevator that led to Todd's apartment and let it carry her up. Once she got to Todd's door she knocked hard, assuming she would have to wake him. Kate stood off to the side of the peep hole so Todd couldn't see that it was her knocking.

Kate waited a minute then knocked again, loudly.

"Okay, Okay, do you know what time it is?" Todd called from the other side of the door.

Todd swung the door open.

"What?" he said angrily and then saw it was Kate. "Oh, it's you."

Todd tried to swing the door closed as he walked away. Kate stopped the door from closing and walked into Todd's apartment.

"Todd, wait, please. I am here to apologize," Kate said.

Todd threw himself onto the couch and glared at Kate.

Kate went over and sat beside Todd on the couch.

"You have been there for me since Jordan's accident, whenever I have needed you," Kate began.

"Yep, that's the thing about being in love with you. You say jump, I say how high," Todd said sounding disgruntled.

"You have been amazing through all of this. You held me when I cried, you forced me to move forward when I couldn't and you pulled me from my self-destruction, when I was ready to explode. The problem is I did explode and I have been angry this whole time. I'm angry at Jordan for leaving me, angry at myself for not loving him the way he deserved, and angry for not living a life that Jordan would be proud of," Kate paused again. "I was not really angry at you for kissing me and saying you were in love with me. It scared me because my feelings for you have changed too. I was confused, and angry for being disloyal to Jordan. I was afraid that I was falling out of love with Jordan because he's been gone so long, and that I was falling in love with you because you have been here. I didn't know how to handle what you were saying so it was easier to blow up the relationship than to deal with my feelings. I was really only mad at myself for thinking I was falling in love with you."

Kate saw Todd straighten when she said the last part.

"My feelings for you did change. You went from being 'Jordan's best friend' to being mine."

"Friend?" Todd ask disgusted by the word.

"Yes Todd, friend, but more than that, you're family. I do love you Todd, more than I ever have. When you told me that you loved me, I just lashed out because I was afraid to really explore what my feelings for you were. I was afraid I was being unfaithful to Jordan."

"Jordan would want you to be happy," Todd pleaded.

"You are right, he might even be okay with me finding love again with you," Kate agreed, "That's not the problem. My accident has caused me to really think about my feelings and how I have behaved and I am so very sorry. You have been here for me, no matter what your motives are. You were here, and you did not deserve how I treated you or anything that I said to you."

"Why do I feel a 'but' coming on?" Todd said sadly.

"I love you Todd, but, my love remains platonic. I am not ready to let go of Jordan. I still believe he is coming back to me," Kate admitted.

"Kate it's almost been a year. How long will it take for you to acknowledge that Jordan is gone?" Todd asked, actually wanting to know an answer.

"I don't know Todd, maybe never. I don't want you sitting and waiting for something that you may never have and miss out on something real with someone else," Kate said thinking of Lily.

"So, you're saying you will never feel about me the way I feel about you?" Todd asked in a whisper.

"No, Todd, I don't think I will. That doesn't mean that I don't care about you, I do. I absolutely do. I do need you in my life, even when Jordan comes back, I am going to need you. We can't go back in time and be who we were before the accident. I don't even think those people exist anymore. If you can't be in my life, I will understand," Kate told him.

Todd leaned in and took Kate's hand, he put it to his cheek and held it there. Kate didn't move or pull away but instead she took her other hand and ran it through his hair.

"I don't know how to let you go," Todd admitted chocking on his words.

"Maybe don't let go, but be my friend," Kate offered.

Todd looked up into her eyes. She could see tears ready to fall. "Okay friend, but I'm going to need a minute to get there."

"Take all the time you need, I will be here when your ready," Kate replied.

They sat there silent for a few minutes looking into each others' eyes.

Kate knew Todd loved her and she loved him but she knew one day Todd would realize that this love was nothing compared to true love, like the love Kate had for Jordan.

"When were you discharged from the hospital? I am surprised Vick didn't tell me," Todd asked, finally breaking the silence.

"Well, I wasn't exactly discharged. I walked out," Kate replied.

"Gees! Kate!" Todd jumped up and pulled her into the spare room, "Rest. We will talk more in the morning," Todd commanded.

Todd wasn't wrong. Kate did feel exhausted but she would have sat there until the end of time if that's how long it took to fix things between Todd and her. The funny thing is Kate didn't fix things with Todd to save Jordan, she fixed things because she wanted to save Todd.

Kate wrapped her arms around Todd's neck and hugged him, "I missed you," she said.

Todd returned her hug.

"Still need a minute Kate," he said as he pulled Kate off him. "Rest," he said.

He turned her to the bed. Kate nodded and did as she was told, feeling like things were on their way to getting back to where they should be. The only thing missing was Jordan.

Chapter 31

Kate was woken by Todd. She could hear him screaming her name from somewhere in the house.

"KATE! Get out of bed!" he yelled.

Kate jumped out of bed and rushed out into the living room to find Todd rushing around.

"What is it? What's wrong? Kate asked worried.

"Where is your cell phone?" Todd asked loudly.

Kate checked her pockets, no cell, and then she recalled she left it in her hospital robe pocket. But what did that matter? She thought.

"I must have forgotten it at the hospital," Kate explained, "Why?" she asked.

"Because, Kate, the hospital has been trying to reach you all morning. They ended up calling Vick, who just called me," Todd said.

Why? Kate wondered to herself still half asleep, and then it hit her like a thunderbolt. JORDAN!

Kate's eyes got big and she stared at Todd, terrified of what was going to come next.

"He's awake, Kate," Todd announced ecstatically, "He's awake!"

It took a few seconds for Kate's brain to process the information.

"Oh, my gosh, oh my gosh," Kate said, in shock.

Kate had dreamed of this day but was losing hope and now that it was here, she was paralyzed. Then it finally sunk in and Kate just fell to her knees, tears pouring down her face.

"Oh, no," Todd said grabbing Kate by the arm and pulling her to her feet, "we do not have time for that," he said.

Todd grabbed Kate by the arm and pulled her right out of the apartment. By the time that they hit the pavement they were both in a flat-out run, jumping into Todd's car. Todd hit the gas, causing the tires to squeal, and Kate saw the cloud of black smoke they left behind. A forty-five-minute drive took ten minutes, and Kate's eyes never left the clock on the dash.

Todd parked the car in a drop off zone.

"It can get towed, I'll deal with that later. I do not want to waste any more time trying to find a parking space," Todd said.

Kate was grateful he was in as much a hurry to get there as she was. They made a mad dash for the door and did not slow down once inside. Kate saw how the people were watching them, probably wondering what had them in such a hurry.

"He's awake!" Kate yelled out and began laughing.

Once they got to the wing Jordan was in they were about to burst into Jordan's room, but a nurse jumped out from behind the desk.

"One at a time," she commanded.

"But..." was all Todd got out of his mouth.

"One at a time and that is final," she said holding her ground.

"Fine. Kate, you go," Todd ushered to Kate.

Kate nodded and rushed into the room and there he was in a seated position, talking to the doctor. Jordan looked at Kate as she came into the room, he's eyes shining with tears when he saw her.

Kate rushed to him, not caring what the doctor was saying. She fell into his embrace and wrapped her own arms around him as tight as she could. Kate could barely believe this was happening. She would cry, then laugh and then cry again. Her tears were tears of joy, tears of relief, tears of who the heck knows and the laughter was releasing a year's worth of tension.

"I'll give you guys a moment," the doctor said and left the room.

It took a long time before either of them could speak or let go.

Jordan was the first to speak, "So, what did I miss?" he asked.

Kate laughing again, "Nothing my love, we were waiting for you," Kate replied.

Kate peeled herself from Jordan's embrace but could not leave his side.

"Do you remember anything from when you were in the coma?" Kate asked, wondering if he remembered Katherine or his glass prison.

"No, I don't," Jordan said, "It was like I passed out in the car and woke up completely fine. It's almost like the car accident was a bad dream, only the doc tells me it's true. The scars are also proof," he said pulling at his gown revealing the puncture wounds he sustained from the accident and the surgery.

Kate sat there staring into Jordan's eyes. It still hurt her to know the pain he must have had in the car. Tears began to fall again.

Jordan wiped them from her face.

"You weren't alone?" Jordan said as a question rather than a statement, "I mean you had Todd and Vick. They were there for you, right?" he asked.

"Absolutely, brother," came a masculine voice. Todd came strolling into the room. The two men looked at each other for a beat and then were embracing.

"Thank goodness, brother, thank goodness," Todd kept saying. They released each other both smiling ear to ear.

This is how it's supposed to be, Kate thought.

"I thought it was one at a time?" Kate asked Todd, happy to have him with them.

"Well, if the nurse comes in, I'll have to hide, or she will have to forcibly remove me. I was not standing in the hall another minute more," Todd replied.

The three of them sat and chatted about things Jordan missed, like the birth of a friend's baby, or an earthquake that happened in another country.

After awhile Jordan told them he was tired and laid back to rest. He was sleeping within minutes. Vick had finally joined them in Jordan's room, just after he fell asleep. Vick dragged in another chair. Kate knew no one was leaving this room until everyone was sure that Jordan was here to stay.

"You weren't here when I got here. Where were you?" Todd asked Vick in a whispered voice.

"Getting this," Vick replied holding up a bottle of whiskey and three plastic cups. "It has been one heck of a year and I think we could all use a drink."

Kate laughed, "That's an understatement."

"Okay, so then we need two drinks. One to take the edge off and one in celebration of Jordan finally coming back to us," Vick said, as he poured the amber liquid in to the cups.

"Cheers," Vick said as he handed out the drinks and threw his back. Todd and Kate followed suit.

The liquor burned her throat but it felt good. It made her realize this was all real.

Vick poured them each another shot.

"Todd, would you like to do the honours?" Vick asked.

Todd nodded.

"Here's to a man, we all love, finding his way back. To friends who made it through the tragedy, that are closer than ever," Todd said, speaking quietly, not wanting to wake Jordan.

"Hear, hear," replied Kate and they all drank.

After a moment, Kate realized there were other people, other friends, who needed to know the good news.

"I don't have my cell phone to let anyone know Jordan is awake," Kate said to Todd and Vick.

Todd pulled out his. "I got this," he said.

"Thanks, can you do me a favour and be sure to let Lily know too," Kate asked.

"Lily? You mean the maid?" Todd questioned arrogantly.

"No, Todd, my friend who works as my cleaner," Kate replied.

"Right," Todd said, "I'm a snob, I will definitely give her a call too."

"Thanks," Kate replied.

Kate sat back in her chair, all the events of the last year weighing on her. She was so exhausted that she passed right out.

Kate dreamed about Katherine. She stood in an open field surrounded by trees and she was embracing John. There was no darkness, there was no glass prison. Katherine looked at Kate.

"Thank you, Kate, for doing what I couldn't," said Katherine.

"Where is Victor?" Kate asked.

"I hope he's moved on, which is where we are headed," replied Katherine.

Then suddenly there was a very bright, blinding light. Kate looked to Katherine.

"This time that had better be for you, because I swear if you hit me again, I am going to haunt your after life," Kate said firmly.

Katherine smiled.

"Yes, Kate, this time it's finally for me," Katherine smiled and faded away.

Chapter 32

Kate woke before Todd and Vick. It took Kate a moment to remember all that had happened. Once she did she quickly looked over at Jordan to see if it was all true. There he was already awake and looking at her.

Kate smiled at Jordan.

"Good morning," Kate said.

"Yes, it is," Jordan replied.

Kate stood, walked over to Jordan's bed and got comfortable laying beside him, his arms wrapped around her. Kate wanted to pinch herself. She just could not believe this was all real and not a dream.

"I have waited for this day, I have dreamed about this day. I am so thankful you finally woke up," Kate said in a hushed voice, so not to wake the others.

"I'm sorry it took me so long," Jordan returned.

"I'm just glad you did. I missed you baby," Kate replied.

Todd and Vick stirred and slowly woke. They both sat up and looked towards Jordan's bed.

"Well, that's a relief," Vick said to Jordan.

"What's a relief?" Jordan asked.

"That I wasn't dreaming, you are awake," Vick said.

"I seem to be getting that lately," Jordan replied giving Kate a poke in the arm.

"So, when do you think you'll get to blow this popsicle stand?" Todd asked.

Jordan shrugged, "Not sure but hopefully soon. I've wasted enough time in here," Jordan replied. "Speaking of, where is the stuff I would have came in with?" he asked.

"What do you mean?" Kate asked.

"My wallet, shoes, underwear, you know my stuff," Jordan said smirking.

"Oh, I have it with my stuff, in my room," Kate said without realizing what just came out of her mouth.

"What do you mean your room? Why were you in the hospital?" Jordan asked concerned.

"I'll tell you all about it another time. I am all good now," Kate said adjusting her head wrap. She was going to have to get those bandages removed.

"Can someone go get the bag for me?" Jordan asked.

Just then, Vick's phone dinged.

"Darn it, I have to go into work, but I will be in and out of here so much you are going to be sick of me," he said pointing a finger at Jordan.

"Looking forward to it," Jordan replied smiling.

"I guess that leaves me. Be right back," Todd said and was off right behind Vick.

Todd returned a few minutes later with both Jordan and Kate's stuff.

"Guess the nurse was happy to clean out your room," Todd said handing over the bags and eyeballing Kate.

Kate squirmed uncomfortably.

"Well, I probably could have handled that better too," she said.

"Yeah, we should know that about you by now," Todd said chuckling.

Jordan looked at Kate questionably

"Something I should know?" he asked.

Kate looked at Jordan, the love of her life, who only deserved to be happy. Todd and Vick made him happy. She knew the events that occurred could hurt their relationships, and she didn't want that.

"Nothing important baby, I may have been a little melodramatic at times, but you know me?" Kate winked at Jordan.

Jordan chuckled, "I sure do," he agreed.

He took the bag and started digging around in it. Once he found what he was looking for he looked to Todd.

"Do you think I could have some time alone with Kate?" Jordan asked.

"Sure thing, brother. I have a job to get to, so I will see you guys later," Todd answered.

Todd turned to leave but before he did, he mouthed the words, thank you, to Kate. She knew it was because Tod she didn't tell Jordan about all that had occurred and she had no plans to ever tell him.

"Finally, we are alone," Jordan breathed.

Kate smiled at him.

"So, I need to talk to you. It was something I was going to discuss with you the night of my accident and never got the chance," Jordan said to Kate.

Kate got a little anxious, what could he need to talk to her about that was still relevant after almost a year.

"We have been together for two years, sorry, three years," Jordan corrected himself. "I was supposed to say this a year ago," he smiled at her apologetically. "I'd been waiting for the right moment to tell you how I feel and never found one. I should have just said it. Just in doing so would have made it the right moment," he said more to himself than her. "Baby, I love you more than words could express and I want to spend my life showing you just how much. Kate Black, will you marry me?" Jordan asked opening the ring box and exposing the ring.

Kate knew the ring was there but never really spent time thinking about what it all meant. She was so busy trying to save Jordan that she didn't really think about the meaning behind the ring. Kate was shocked and gasped in surprise. She was stunned silent. They had never talked about marriage and what that would look like, but she knew there would never be anyone else.

"Baby? Do you have anything you'd like to say?" Jordan coaxed.

"Yes," Kate said crying, "yes, yes, yes, yes, yes," she said and Jordan pulled her into his arms and kissed her, and she kissed him with everything she had.

Their lip lock lasted a long time. After all, they had plenty to make up for. After they emerged from the kiss, Kate curled up with Jordan on his bed, listening to his heart beat. It felt so good to be here again. Kate recalled her dream of Katherine in the field and the bright light. Kate knew that the past had been righted. She had never felt more complete then she did right now.

The Doctor came in to speak with Jordan, but Kate did not move from Jordan's side. She wasn't going to move an inch, whether the doctor liked it or not.

The doctor looked at Kate, seemed to understand, and turned back to Jordan.

"Well, Mr. Best, you had me stumped at times but I am very happy to say that I see no reason to keep you here much longer. I'd like to run a few more tests tomorrow and I suspect they will all be fine. You will find yourself home in your own bed within the next few days," he announced.

Jordan thanked him for all he did and the doctor left.

"Did you hear that?" Jordan asked Kate.

"Yes," Kate said, "you're going home," she said happily.

"No, not that," Jordan replied.

Kate pulled herself away and peered up into Jordan's eyes.

"He said bed," Jordan replied wriggling his eyebrows at Kate.

Kate squirmed. The thought of making love to him again was conflicting. It was the farthest thing from her mind but now hearing him say it made her not want to wait. It had been so long, she was worried they would not be in sync, but they never would be if they didn't try.

"Well, I hate to be the one to point out the obvious but we are on one now," Kate teased.

Adrianna Cote

"So, it would seem," Jordan began, "but I am weak, I did just wake from a coma," he teased back.

Kate pulled herself up onto all fours straddling Jordan.

"I guess I'll have to do all the work," Kate said sighing.

Jordan grabbed Kate by the shirt and yanked her on top of him, "looks liked," he agreed.

Jordan touched his lips to hers, then they were lost and all that existed was the two of them and their bodies reconnecting after all this time.

Chapter 33

It was a sunny summer day, and it was hotter than heck. His sister, Lily, had dragged him to her boss's wedding. It was too freaking hot to be in a black suit and tie. Who has a wedding outside in this heat, he thought to himself disgruntled.

"Come on Lenny," Lily said pulling on his arm.

They hurried up the lush green lawn and found their seats. The wedding ceremony was taking place in a chapel garden. The guests were surrounded by tall bushes that sprouted all different types and colours of flowers. The alter was wrapped in white tulle and flowers. Aside from the location, it was quite simple. Not what Lenny would have expected from this uptown bunch of people.

A tall burley guy stood to the right of the alter and when he saw them come in, a huge grin became plastered on his face. Lenny knew the guy. That was the new guy Lily was dating. Lily seemed happy, which, he really could care less about. As long as Lily stayed out of his way he didn't care.

Lenny didn't care about many people and he cared very little for Lily, even though they were supposedly twins. Their dad had told them they were twins, but as they grew up Lenny became suspicious. Lenny and Lily did not look alike, not even a little, they had no shared interests. They were in every way polar opposites.

Lenny would eavesdrop on his parent's conversations to see if he could find out some clue as to why he was so different from Lily. He never found anything out, until the day his mother died. That was the day she pulled Lenny aside and told him the truth. So, armed with the truth, Lenny began to follow his dad when he went out every night. Lenny quickly became aware of his father's skeletons. He would quietly watch from a hiding spot, until one day he was found by his father.

Lenny got a severe beating but after that his father brought Lenny with him to teach him all his secrets. Then one day his father had a heart attack and died as he was playing with his toys. Lenny had to drag his father's dead body from their secret spot to the car and drive him to get medical attention, knowing it was a ruse. From that day forward his father's secret became only Lenny's.

Lenny never told Lily about what he learned. Lily was useful, in that she helped pay the bills, so he could have more time to play, which seemed like a good trade off. Lenny wasn't going to let anything get in his way, that included Lily. Lenny would deal with her if he had to.

Lily on the other hand was none the wiser and believed whatever she was told. She was naive and gullible and loved Lenny as she should love a brother. Lenny milked that for all it was worth but at times Lily was so darn irritating, like when she dragged him to this stupid wedding.

"I have to use the can," Lenny announced to Lily then got up to leave.

Lenny hated weddings. It was ridiculous to think someone could love you forever, but you could darn well make them stay forever. You didn't need a piece of paper or God for that, and that was the commandment Lenny lived by.

Lenny looked around the room checking out the women in their fancy attire. He was curious to find his next playmate, but none were to his liking. He continued to peruse to no avail. He returned to his seat beside Lily, missing the bride's walk down the aisle. Too bad, Lenny thought sarcastically.

To the right of the bride was a small brunette. Lenny couldn't see what she looked like and she never turned around. She probably wasn't right anyway. This crowd didn't seem to suit him but the tattoo between her shoulder blades made Lenny curious about her. It was a simple tattoo of angel wings that an uptown girl would never show off at such a formal affair.

The bride and groomed kissed and everyone clapped and stood. Lenny did as well, strictly for show. The happy couple headed back up the aisle and Lenny got a good look at the bride. She was hot, too bad she was married. One thing about Lenny, he wasn't interested in married women, he could literally smell the second-hand odour coming off them. Lenny turned back to the front hoping to catch a look at the brunette but she had disappeared.

Lenny smiled, so she was playing hide and seek. I like games Lenny thought, more so, I like to win. This wedding just became more interesting.

* * * * * *

Jenny stepped out the back door to call the hotel and set up the finishing touches on the room she had gotten for Jordan and Kate's wedding night. Once in their room, Jordan and Kate would find the trip to paradise for two, courtesy of Todd.

Jenny was Todd and Vick's younger sister. She only came to town occasionally. Her home was in France, but Jordan getting married brought her home. Jordan was like another brother to her and she wanted to be here for him and Kate. If any two-people deserved happiness it was the two of them.

Jenny hoped that one day she will find someone to love and who will love her the way Jordan and Kate loved each other, but she wasn't holding out for it. Jenny finished her call with the concierge and shoved her phone back in her purse.

She headed into the kitchen to check in with the cook. She wanted to see what time he'd be ready to serve dinner, a task Jenny regretted the moment she stepped foot in the kitchen.

"De shrimp were late, dey came in wit my sous chef!" he shouted in his French accent.

"Okay, okay I was just looking for a time not a tear down," Jenny replied.

"Pardon," the chef said with a huff, "I will let you know," he said waving her off.

Jenny shrugged and headed out to the bar, in need of a drink. She ordered a shot of tequila and then a glass of wine. She sat and watched all the guests laughing and drinking, happy to celebrate this day with Jordan and Kate.

Jenny finally located Todd, he had one arm wrapped around Lily and the other was shaking hands. She was happy Todd had been pushed into Lily's arms. The girl looks at him like he hung the moon. Todd was her brother and she wanted him to be ridiculously happy. She downed the last of her wine and grabbed another for the road, deciding it was time to mingle. She was told weddings were a great place to meet someone, so she headed off in search of a body to keep her bed warm that night.

* * * * * *

Kate and Jordan headed into the bridal suite so they could be alone. They had spent all morning taking pictures and had just enough time to make it to the church before the wedding march began. Kate wasn't a superstitious person so Jordan seeing her before the wedding meant very little to her. What meant more was lying in his arms every night for the rest of her life.

Kate was wrapped in Jordan's arm and they were locked in a passionate kiss. He had backed her against a wall and was trying to find her under her dress. Kate jumped out of his arms.

"Oh, no, it took an army of women to get me into this thing, and I only get to wear it for one day, so it is not coming off any time soon," Kate said holding Jordan at arms length.

"That's alright, I can work with that," Jordan laughed and tugged at her skirt.

258

Kate squealed and ran to the door. The dress as beautiful as it was, weighed a ton and slowed her down. Jordan had her in his arms again before Kate's was able to grab the door knob.

"Where are you off to Mrs. Best?" Jordan asked.

Mmmmm, Kate moaned to herself, Mrs. Best. Kate liked the sound of that.

"Well, Mr. Best, we have a room full of guests waiting for our grand entrance," Kate replied.

Jordan dipped Kate and kissed her right above the heart. It sent shivers through her and she moaned out loud.

"Don't do that Mrs. Best, or I can't be held accountable for what I do next," Jordan said with his 'I'm serious' face.

"What you are going to do next is kiss your wife, and the mother of your child, and then walk her into that room because she is famished," Kate replied showing Jordan her 'serious face.'

"Wait, what?" Jordan asked, "don't you mean future mother of my children?"

"Yes, that's what I mean, in about 8 months' time," Kate said and started laughing.

"What!" Jordan said shocked and picked her up into his embrace, twirling her around. "This is amazing! I'm going to be a dad! Wait," he paused, "but when?"

"I'm going with the night you proposed and nurse Peters walked in," Kate chuckled.

Jordan laughed too. "Yeah, she was pretty upset. So, a dad?" Jordan said.

"A great dad," Kate replied.

Jordan began kissing Kate and the heat between them grew. Kate pushed Jordan so his lips parted just enough from hers.

"Um, eating for two now, very hungry," Kate said.

Jordan released Kate, "Whatever you need, my love."

Jordan paused and put a hand over her belly.

"My loves," he said his smile widening into a big toothy grin.

Jordan opened the door and they headed off to begin their life as man and wife.

Epilogue

Todd stood, shaking hands with person after person, a smile on his face, but he was over this whole thing. He wasn't much for weddings and he hated sticking around for the reception, but he did for two reasons, one, his best friends were the bride and groom and two, his girl wanted to dance.

"Are we talking bumping and grinding, because then I'm in" Todd asked Lily, when she insisted they would stay the whole night to dance.

Lily had punched him on the arm.

"Don't be crude," she scolded him. "I want a slow dance, I want to be wrapped up in your arms," she said batting her eyelashes at him, "and then yes, a bump and grind."

Lily winked and bumped Todd with her hip for emphasis.

Todd never thought he would ever find someone after Kate, but fate had put him in front of this amazing woman. Sure, he was put off at first because Lily was a maid, but after a while it began to appeal to him. Sexy French maid and all, but what got him was she was okay with the fact that Todd's mind worked that way.

This woman got him like no other. She was never put off by his absolute thirst for sex, and she gave as much as she gets. Todd never thought he would ever find someone he could be real with. He didn't even think he would have been able to be himself with Kate. It felt good to be loved for who you were and not who you were pretending to be.

"Woman, don't start things you can't finish!" Todd scolded.

"Who says I can't," Lily said lifting her eyebrow.

Todd was about to scoop her up when another man came up to them, Todd held out his hand and introduced himself.

"No need to be formal, Todd, this is my twin brother Lenny," Lily said introducing them.

It struck Todd as weird, that Lily and Lenny didn't look alike at all. He wouldn't have even thought them to be related. Todd shook Lenny's hand. He always took his first impressions from a hand shake even when he met women. Todd liked a person with a firm grasp that would match his arm pump. Lenny's was limp and soft.

Todd got a weird vibe from this guy, but he was going to keep his feelings to himself because trashing her brother could make things a tad complex between him and Lily. Todd wasn't ready for their first fight, although he would quite enjoy it when they made up. Speaking of, Todd thought.

"It was nice to meet you, if you will just excuse us there is something we need to attend to," Todd said and walked away pulling Lily behind him.

"What do we have to attend to?" Lily asked confused.

"I believe the words bump and grind were used," Todd said winking at her.

Lily chuckled, "well then, after you," and they disappeared from the hall.

******

Lenny watched Lily and Todd leave. He didn't like this Todd guy, he had a feeling he was going to be trouble. Lenny was going to have to do something about this relationship before things got too far.

"Oh, where are they going? I was just about to talk to them?" came a female voice.

Lenny turned to see who the voice belonged to. It was the small brunette he'd been looking for since the ceremony. 1,2,3 on you, he thought to himself.

She was a looker, with a great figure. Lenny liked a more athletic build. She had wide shoulders and just the right amount of cleavage. She had the aura of uptown girl but he saw the rebellion in the tattoos she proudly showed off.

"Not sure," Lenny said, "something about having to tend to something,"

The female shrugged, "Oh, well, I'm Jenny Oak. Todd there is my brother."

Lenny thought about that for a second, Lily hadn't mention Todd had a sister.

"Lenny," he replied, "I am Lily's twin brother"

"Twin, wow. I mean that's cool, but you guys look nothing alike?" Jenny commented.

Yeah, a girl who speaks her mind, this chick was getting better and better Lenny thought.

"Yeah, we get that a lot. Lily never mentioned Todd had a sister, just a brother, Nick. Are you it or are there more siblings?" Lenny asked

"It's Vick. And no just Vick, Todd and I," Jenny replied. "Well it was nice meeting you. I'll see you around."

Jenny waved and was off.

Lenny watched as Jenny walked away. She was everything he liked in a woman and vowed that she would be his next playmate. Oh yes, sweet thing, I will see you around, and I will make you mine, Lenny thought to himself.

"Yes, yes you will be mine," Lenny said aloud.

Confirming to himself that getting Jenny was next on his bucket list, only his hostel had no vacancies at the moment. So, someone was going to have to go in order to make room for his next conquest. The question was who would he have to give up to make room for Jenny? Talia? Megan? Charlotte? No not charlotte. Brigitte.... Yes, Brigitte has lost her shine.

"Bye-bye Bridgett and hello Jenny, Lenny said in her direction. Lenny was finally enjoying the wedding.

Check out my Facebook page for updates and new release dates.

https://www.facebook.com/FindingStrongerRoots/

I love to hear your thoughts on my novels and characters. Please feel free to post on my Facebook page or reviews on the bookstore you purchased from.

You can also subscribe to get updates on what's happening or for new release dates. Check out my website.

https://www.adriannacote.ca

www.ingramcontent.com/pod-product-compliance
Lightning Source LLC
Chambersburg PA
CBHW031308170626
46807CB00001B/333